She said, "Shell, don't rush me," and then we were pressed together. I rested my hands on her shoulders and then let them slide down her back.

And damned if she didn't scoot out of my clutches and tear across the floor. It was the prettiest sight you ever did see, but it wasn't what I'd been led to expect.

I tore after her, but just as I got everything all fixed up, she wriggled away again. All this running was beginning to tell on me, but she seemed good for several more miles. I was beginning to think that was all she was good for.

She was a clever girl, though. She knew that the way to a man's heart was not through his stomach, but through his eyeballs. She stopped running and came walking toward me, slowly, hips swaying, everything swaying.

"You're trying to sway me," I said, "but I warn you, I intend to be firm."

"Good," she sighed. "I'm not going anywhere."

Another one for *Tina*

Other Original Gold Medal Novels by

Richard S. Prather:

BODIES IN BEDLAM
CASE OF THE VANISHING BEAUTY
FIND THIS WOMAN
WAY OF A WANTON
EVERYBODY HAD A GUN
DARLING, IT'S DEATH
TOO MANY CROOKS
STRIP FOR MURDER
THE WAILING FRAIL
THREE'S A SHROUD
HAVE GAT—WILL TRAVEL
TAKE A MURDER, DARLING
SLAB HAPPY

Always Leave 'Em Dying

An Original Gold Medal Novel by

Richard S. Prather

Gold Medal Books

FAWCETT PUBLICATIONS, INC.
FAWCETT BLDG., FAWCETT PLACE, GREENWICH, CONN.

Chapter One

L ET ME OUT of this thing!" I yelled.

The shapely psychiatrist, the two doctors, both burly guards—everybody ignored me. The strait jacket's canvas held my arms tight. My wrenched shoulder ached. My head ached. My back ached. Hell, I ached all over.

My six-two was horizontal on a stretcher and the two bruisers carried it and my 205 pounds easily down the long corridor. I was as confused as modern art, and being in this stupid insane asylum didn't help.

Consciousness had just returned and my eyes wouldn't yet focus properly, but I could see the two doctors, Wolfe and Yancey, walking at the left side of the stretcher. I shouted at them, "What the hell is this? Are you damn fools part of the staff, or patients? I'm Shell Scott, a private detective. And I'm not crazy. Do I look crazy?"

They didn't even glance around. Maybe that was the wrong thing to ask them, anyway. Inch-long white hair sticking up in the air like a scalp-sized cowlick, peculiarly angled whitish eyebrows, and a slightly bent nose may not be glamour, but they're no indication of cackling gray matter.

I turned my head to the right side of the stretcher and there in her starched white uniform was the lovely little psychiatrist with the shape that should have unstarched her uniform, and my eyes suddenly focused improperly. The stretcher veered left. I was carried into a room, lights blazed, and I was dumped unceremoniously onto a narrow bed, yelling like a fiend.

Dr. Wolfe stared down at me, light glancing from rimless glasses perched on his bulbous nose. He looked like a silver-eyed owl as he said, "He's getting violent again." He left, returned shortly with a gleaming hypodermic syringe in one hand. I felt a stinging sensation as the needle entered my neck.

5

Seconds later the light flicked out and all of them left the room. The door slammed shut and I was alone in darkness. All those characters thought I was goofy. Either that, I groaned to myself, or the inmates had taken over the asylum. The drug had started taking effect almost at once and I fought to keep from going to sleep; but finally I let my eyelids close. There was a soft, sharp clicking sound and I forced my eyes open. Somebody stepped inside my room, then pushed the door shut again. A thin beam of light shot from a small flashlight held in the person's hand. Reflections sparkled from a large diamond ring on one finger of the other hand—and on something that was gripped in those fingers, some kind of blade, long, sharp-edged, like a knife or scalpel.

"Hey," I said thickly, my voice sounding muffled. "What the hell—"

There was a muttered curse, and light flashed upon my face. The blade moved upward through the beam of light. And suddenly I was wide awake, thinking: This idiot is about to stab me.

The rest of it was just sound and movement. The yelling I had done before was nothing compared to this; everybody in the cackle factory must have heard me. I jerked my body aside, the jacket binding me, got my heels hooked over the bed's edge, and rolled. The blade sliced across my back as I strained my leg muscles and felt myself slide, then fall to the floor. I rolled onto my back and drew up my legs to kick at the figure above me, but the flashlight winked out and the figure jumped past me. I heard a scraping sound like that of a window being raised.

Rapid footsteps slapped in the corridor outside. The door opened again and lights blazed. A strange nurse stood in the doorway, blinking. Feet pounded in the hall and one of the guards came inside, then the little psychiatrist and another doctor. Hands lifted me to the bed again as Dr. Yancey came in, followed by Dr. Wolfe and another man. People were babbling at me. I babbled right back at them, much louder than they: "You've got a nut running around loose. Tried to stab me. Get this goddamned jacket off me."

Dr. Yancey said slowly, soothingly, "We don't have any homicidal cases here."

"That's what *you* think." My thoughts were blurred, my muscles leaden from the drug. "I tell you, somebody tried to kill me. Went out the window."

The psychiatrist pressed a cool hand on my forehead. "Don't get excited," she said. "You must have dreamed it."

"The hell I dreamed it!"

They all moved away from my bed and the light went out. The door closed and I was alone again, warm wetness beneath me from blood draining through the cut in my back.

The pulse beat heavily in my temples. I knew I could yell my head off now and nobody would come. And I knew that too many crazy things had happened too quickly here tonight. It might not have been a maniac at all that had tried to kill me. Maybe this had happened because of the case I was on, because of something I'd done earlier today. Maybe somebody very sane, and frightened, wanted me dead. I thought back to this morning, when it had begun. I felt my eyes closing and forced them open, kept them stretched wide in the darkness.

Chapter Two

It was one of those rare, completely smog-free days when you can see Los Angeles from Los Angeles. Often you can't find City Hall unless you're in it, but this was one of those mornings when you spring out of bed nearly overwhelmed by oxygen.

I sprang all over my three-rooms-and-bath in Hollywood's Spartan Apartment Hotel. I felt so good that I didn't even mind when the phone rang and I wound up with a client, despite the fact that this was the early A.M. of a Sunday, my downtown L.A. office was closed, and I was supposed to be gathering strength to face Monday.

The gal on the phone was a Mrs. Gifford, she had a missing daughter and was greatly worried, and would I try to find the daughter? Sure, today I'd find anything. I felt swell clear out to East Los Angeles, but some of the bubbles went out of me when I found the address I wanted and parked. This was a run-down, kind of sleazy section of town, and even before I started up the walk, I could hear a TV set blaring from inside the house: "Stomach tied in knots? Try GUTBALM!" I rang the doorbell anyway.

Somebody yelled for me to come in. All the blinds were drawn and no lights were on in the front room, but by estimating direction and distance from a glowing TV set, I found Mrs. Gifford. She was sagging on a couch, fat spilling over the borders of a faded housecoat, worn slippers on her feet. Her face looked like something a baker might have made of dough: two fingers poked into it for eyes, a tweak in the middle for a nose, and the side of a hand slammed into it for a mouth; from there several chins were terraced toward a thick neck.

Despite the fact that half the time she was giving her attention to the TV set, I learned that Mrs. Gifford had divorced her husband when Felicity, their only child, was about a year old; she'd got custody of the girl, who was sixteen now. For a few minutes she explained how fortunate it was that she'd got "my little girl" away from the eight kinds of fiend she claimed her husband had been. I gathered that hubby had been a lusty cat, perhaps not very honest, who'd chased around with some other women; Mrs. Gifford intimated that she'd caught him at it. While she suffered audibly, I wondered what I was doing here. Finally she brought me up to date.

Saturday night about nine-thirty, Felicity had answered the phone, talked briefly, and scribbled on a writing pad, then had hung up and sat quietly for several minutes, doodling on the tablet. She'd then told her mother good night, gone to her room, and, presumably, crawled into bed. But in the morning Felicity had been gone. The bed hadn't been slept in, and Mrs. Gifford hadn't seen or heard from her daughter since.

I asked her, "Police know about this yet?"

"Yes. I talked to them already, the Missing People persons. But they got so many to look for and all, I phoned you."

"Uh-huh." Missing Persons would do most of the things I could do. And this deal sounded like a dozen cases I'd had in the past; gals get fed up or want a fling for any of a hundred reasons, and take off. Usually you find them in a couple of days—if they haven't already come back home, not much older but usually wiser.

I said, "Has Felicity ever run away before?"

"Oh, no. And she didn't run away, I know that. Felicity wouldn't run away. Something terrible must of happened."

8

"I mean, she apparently left under her own power. She could hardly have been forced out of her own bedroom."

Mrs. Gifford shook her head and said doggedly, "Something terrible must of happened."

"You know who called her last night?"

"No. I supposed it was one of her girl friends. Don't know anybody else it could of been. You think that had anything to do with it?"

"I don't know." For all I knew, the gal might have eloped with the captain of the football team, but I didn't burden Mrs. Gifford with that thought. "If you'll give me a list of their names," I said, "I'll check with them. Better list any boy friends who might have phoned."

"It wouldn't of been a boy, Mr. Scott."

"I mean, since it was Saturday night, maybe it was just some kid trying to make a date."

Mrs. Gifford rolled her eyes toward the ceiling and laughed softly. "Oh, my goodness," she said in a tone she might have reserved for idiots, "you don't suppose my little girl goes out with boys! She's just a child, you know."

I grinned. "Sorry. I thought you said she was sixteen."

The dough of Mrs. Gifford's face seemed to settle and harden. She said in a flat, quiet voice, "Felicity is sixteen, Mr. Scott. A child of that age can't possibly know how to protect herself against men. I'd be failing in my duty as a mother if I didn't protect her from being hurt."

She had spoken quietly, with the assurance of a settled and unarguable conviction. While she looked at me with a slight frown on her heavy face, I remembered what she'd told me about her ex-husband. Her violence when she'd spoken of him made me wonder if she hated him as much as she'd professed to, or resented him, or just felt mean this morning. Anyway, she'd been hurt; she was going to make very sure her daughter wasn't hurt. The hell of it was she probably thought she could do it.

For the first time I began to think of Felicity as something more than just another case. I wondered what she was like, where she was, and if she were O.K.

I said, "Of course. You mentioned that Felicity wrote something on a pad by the phone. Could I take a look?"

Mrs. Gifford craned her head toward a small table, bare except for a French phone, then frowned and said, "I don't rightly remember, but I think maybe she took it to the bedroom with her." She was silent for several seconds, then sighed. "I better go look, I guess."

After she heaved herself off the couch I followed her across a narrow hall, then into a small bedroom, which she said was Felicity's. While she hunted for the writing pad, I looked around. Everything was as neatly in place as a balding man's hairs, and it wasn't until I saw how neat and clean Felicity's room was that I became conscious of disarray and untidiness in the rest of the house. That comparison, though, was only preparation for what was something of a shock for me.

On an unpainted pine dresser were several brushes and combs, a pair of scissors, and a hand-tinted photographic portrait in a cardboard frame. The picture was of a young girl with a heart-shaped face, heavy dark brows arched above big, widely spaced eyes, lips curved slightly in a smile. It was the portrait of an attractive young girl on the verge of becoming a beautiful woman, and I suppose it was because I had been so little impressed by Mrs. Gifford that it didn't occur to me that the picture might be of Felicity.

It was, though, as Mrs. Gifford told me when I casually asked. I picked up the portrait and looked at it. The big eyes were dark, long-lashed, and she had boyishly short dark hair. Her front teeth were slightly crooked, but it didn't hurt her nice smile. She wore no make-up.

Mrs. Gifford closed a drawer behind me. "Here it is," she said. "Nothing on it."

I turned around and she handed me the pad. The top sheet was blank, but by holding the tablet so that light struck its surface at a shallow angle I could make out the indentations of three words, beneath which the paper was covered with marks of doodling, swirls and circles.

I said, "Looks like she wrote down, 'Dixon—Birch and Ivy,' then tore off the top sheet. That mean anything to you?"

She shook her head, chins swaying, then frowned. "Oh, Birch and Ivy. That's an intersection a little ways from here. A block up—" she pointed—"and three down."

Mrs. Gifford looked over Felicity's belongings at my request. The girl had apparently taken nothing with her except her purse and the clothes she'd been wearing Friday night: white blouse, gray sweater and skirt, low-heeled black shoes.

Mrs. Gifford said, "You want anything else in here?"

"I'd like to look around a little more, if it's O.K."

10

"You go ahead, Mr. Scott." She nodded, went back into the front room.

I spent another ten minutes snooping, and it was oddly embarrassing to look at Felicity's intimate belongings, books and trinkets, souvenirs. But I wanted to know as much about her as I could. L.A. is big, and a little gal could easily lose herself in it. I wanted to know as much as possible about the way she lived.

The few things I'd learned about Mrs. Gifford had told me quite a bit about what her daughter might be like; the neat, clean room told me a little more. The clothing was all drab, mostly dark blues and grays; there was one pair of brown low-heeled shoes and a brown cloth coat. The only bright colors I found were two hair ribbons, one yellow, one red. There were four school textbooks, a Bible, a well-thumbed volume of hymns, and six movie magazines. I found an almost full bottle of bright-red nail polish, but it was in a peculiar place, in the dresser's bottom drawer under some handkerchiefs. After I'd thumbed through the few snapshots I found, Felicity by herself or with other young girls plus a couple of snaps of other girls alone, I went back into the front room.

Seated alongside Mrs. Gifford again, in front of the TV set, I asked, "Is there any chance Felicity might simply have stayed at a girl friend's house?"

"She wouldn't of done that."

"Was there any indication that she might have been planning something like this? Could she have been thinking of running away? To friends out of town, anything?"

"Why would she run away?"

For a couple of seconds I felt like giving this gal a straight answer to that question, but I let it pass and said, "She seem happy, normal? Health good?"

Mrs. Gifford thought about it. "Oh, she seemed a little nervous-like lately. Skittery. And she wasn't feeling none too well, sickly most of the time, upset stomach." Stumick, she said.

"How long had she been like that?"

"Oh, two or three months, I guess. It's hard to say, exactly, I've been feeling so poorly myself."

"Uh-huh. Had she been to a doctor?"

"No. It wasn't nothing serious, just part of growing up."

"I see." I reached for cigarettes, then changed my mind. There weren't any ash trays in the house, and it seemed a safe bet that Mrs. Gifford didn't smoke. "Just a thought," I said, "but is there any chance that Felicity was pregnant?" I barely got the last word out.

"What a *terrible* thing to say!" Mrs. Gifford gasped. Her eyes got wide and her mouth got small, and through almost closed lips she said, angrily, "Why, that's impossible. Felicity don't know the first thing about . . . about sex. You shouldn't even suggest—"

"I'm sorry. I don't mean to be offensive, but I've got to ask any questions that might conceivably be important. Felicity's illness, and her—"

"Now, that's enough! She's not that kind of a girl at all. I've taken good care of her."

"Sure, Mrs. Gifford. Sorry I mentioned it. I get used to all sorts of angles in my job, and I thought maybe—"

"She's a *good* girl, Mr. Scott. Why, she's a Trammelite."

"She's a what?"

"A Trammelite. She goes and listens to Mr. Trammel 'most every night."

Those words rang a bell; a rather cracked bell, at that. And I didn't like the sound of it. Trammelites were devotees of Trammelism, a crackpot cult built on the mouthings of one Arthur Trammel. I knew quite a bit about Trammel, had met him, and I figured if he kept on the way he was going, he might eventually succeed in disorganizing as many minds as organized religion. Most of his followers were odd balls to begin with, and after listening to him a while, they usually wound up as warped as Trammel. If Felicity were mixed up with that bunch, I wanted to know all about it.

"Your daughter spent a lot of time at Trammelite meetings?"

"Oh, yes. She even sung in the choral group Mr. Trammel has. Only twenty of them, and she's one. They sing beautiful."

"You've heard them yourself at meetings, huh?"

"Many a time. I've gone there many a time just to hear him. Mr. Trammel is a wonderful man, isn't he?"

A wonderful man, I thought, who'll put clothes on fish the first chance he gets. "I was thinking," I said, "that some of the Trammelites might be able to help us. It's possible one of them might know something about where Felicity could be, since she spent so much time at meetings."

Mainly I was poking around for more information, but Mrs. Gifford nodded her head. "I never thought of that.

But, you know, that's true. If anybody would know, it would be them. Almost all her friends and people she knows, they're Trammelites, too, the best people. And Mr. Trammel—" She stopped.

"Yes?" I tried to smile pleasantly. "Mr. Trammel?"

She nibbled on her lip, then lowered her voice. "He knows things . . . things ordinary people don't."

"He does?" I waited for more, but that was all she cared to say. I didn't like a bit of it, either. It looked as though, if I started talking to people Felicity knew, trying to hunt her down, I'd run into little but Trammelites. That could make this a tougher job than it should have been. If I banged up against a flock of Trammel's peculiar followers, anything might happen; it was even possible that their leader himself might have a stroke. I lit a cigarette, and the hell with Mrs. Gifford, while I thought a while about what this might have to do with Felicity and my search for her.

In and around L.A. there are more square crackpots per mile than in any other place you can name. We've got literally hundreds of cults—everything from John Believer's World Security Party, with its devilishly clever slogan, "Everybody Is Something," to Zoomites, complete with Head Zoom—and of all the cults, Arthur Trammel's is the biggest, best known, and most profitable. He'd been in operation only about two years, but in that short time his followers had grown from a handful to tentfuls—partly because he'd gathered around him half a dozen sharp characters who helped him run the operation and who, with Trammel, were called the Guardians, but mainly because he was such a smooth-voiced, brainy con man.

I hated Arthur Trammel. I hated his ugly face, his ugly mind, and practically everything he stood for or against or even near. He was a self-appointed and self-satisfied censor who could dream up more sins to stamp out than you could shake a naughty finger at. You know the type, one of those joyless sonsofbitches who'll make you do what they think is good for you if it kills you. I'd known enough about the guy to hate him even before I'd met him, but meeting him was the clincher.

A few months back he'd come to my office and tried to hire me. He wanted me to find a library; the Guardians' entire collection of pornography had been stolen. Trammel told me the library was maintained only as, in his own words, "a standard with which current filth in bookstores and on newsstands" could be compared. Which explained, he said, why they wanted it back; their standard was gone. Also, he told me solemnly, there was a danger that the books might fall into the wrong hands.

I laughed till I damn near slid off my chair, then told Trammel I wouldn't look for his library, wouldn't throw him a cork if he were sinking in a sewer, and that I hoped he fell down the stairs when he left my office, which he was about to do, and which he did. I hadn't seen him since. I didn't really want to.

But I said to Mrs. Gifford, "I might want to talk with Mr. Trammel. Can you think of anything else that might help me?" There was a long ash on my cigarette, so I flipped it into my coat pocket.

Mrs. Gifford gave me a couple of snapshots of her daughter and made a list for me including names of Felicity's girl friends, her school address, and her teachers. It was a long list; maybe Felicity's friends were all girls, but she had a lot of them.

Almost as an afterthought I told Mrs. Gifford my usual fee for a day's work, and she nearly sprang off the couch. There is no point in describing what followed, but I got the impression this flabby bag had expected to hire me for a nickel a day, or else assumed—logically enough, after twenty years of it—that the government would pay for everything out of taxes. One of the more coherent things she cried was "I got nothing but the alimony," after which we settled my fee. She could pay me "a hundred dollars at the uppermost," and I told her that was dandy, and left. By that time all I wanted was to get out of there.

My black Caddy convertible was parked at the curb, gleaming. It purred softly as I drove away. The sky was still blue, the air fresh and clear, and it was another lousy day.

Chapter Three

AN HOUR LATER I was in my office in downtown L.A. and had most of my lines out. I'd checked with Missing Persons, hospitals, bus and train stations, made a lot of phone calls. I'd phoned most of the people whose names Mrs.

Gifford had listed for me, and learned quite a bit more about Felicity—but without getting even a hint of what might have happened to her, where she might be, or why she was missing.

Before that hour was up I had a couple of other guys working on the case for me—which bright idea was probably going to cost me at least the hundred bucks I was supposed to get for this job. It didn't make good sense, not only because that's no way to run a business, but because I hadn't even met Felicity. I was getting worried about the little gal, though.

Maybe the difference this time was Mrs. Gifford herself; maybe it was seeing that portrait of Felicity when I'd expected someone quite different. But I think mainly it was the way people spoke of her. Everybody I'd talked to on the phone obviously liked her; not one had anything bad to say about her, and most expressed quick concern at the thought that something might have happened to her.

Some of their remarks had made my mental image of Felicity more vivid, too, and I could almost imagine her rapid walk, her soft, quiet voice in conversation. I knew that she always had a scrubbed-clean look, was even-tempered and quick to smile, bit her nails, sang almost nightly in the Trammelite choir. She was brainy, too, up at the top of her class, according to a teacher I'd talked to. I'd got an over-all impression of a sweet, quiet little gal, somewhat shy, keeping pretty much to herself except for her activity in the Trammelite group, which seemed to be her one big interest. I couldn't help wondering what kind of girl she must be that so many people would, without a single exception, speak so well of her.

There were a few people on Mrs. Gifford's list whom I hadn't called. I wanted to talk to some of Felicity's friends in person, so I locked the office and took off. The next hour or so, unfortunately, taught me more about Trammelites and their leader than about Felicity.

In the various L.A. cults, I'd seen practically every type of humanity imaginable, and some of them even looked normal, but there was almost always something unhinged somewhere, or they wouldn't have been cultists. Practically none of the groups I'd been up against before was like any other, but they'd all had one thing in common: They were all against sin, and none of them could define it. Naturally, they had their own sect's definition, and naturally, it disagreed with everybody else's. Most of them could beat their wives on Friday, make love to the chickens on Saturday, but be right up front on Sunday, singing "Open the Gates and Let Me In."

The Trammelites weren't an exception. I had guessed that from the tone of several phone conversations, but it was more obvious out among them. Many were pleasant, some were even enjoyable, but they were still Trammelites, and it showed. Mary Lewis was one of the milder examples.

She was a tall, slim girl about Felicity's age, with black hair pulled tight behind her head, and thin, unpainted lips. I sat in the living room with her and Mrs. Lewis, who watched me closely. Mary was saying, "I just can't understand it. I wondered why she didn't call me last night. Golly, I hope nothing's wrong."

"Did she say she'd call you?"

"Well, no, I just thought we'd be at the meeting together. We both sing in the choral group. When she wasn't there, I wondered why she hadn't called me. I thought she was maybe sick, is all. Golly."

"You didn't phone her last night?" She shook her head and I said, "Somebody did. Felicity wrote some names on a pad by the phone. Birch and Ivy—an intersection near her home—and the name Dixon. You have any idea what that would mean?"

Mary shook her head again, eyes worried.

"She act any different lately? Seem the same as always to you?"

"Just the same. She wouldn't say anything if she was dying, anyway. She's like that. But I didn't notice . . ." Mary paused momentarily, then went on: "I did see her going to the Healing Room the first of last week. I'd forgotten. She was going home with me after the meeting, but then she said she couldn't. I just happened to see her going in there. Golly."

"The what room? The Healing Room? What's that?"

Mary smiled thinly. "I keep forgetting you aren't a Trammelite, Mr. Scott." She sounded sorry for me. "The All-High receives there any of us in need of help or advice. He is always available to any of us, and no problem is too small. He is such a good man, a wise man."

Her voice had dropped lower, become more hushed as she spoke of the All-High, and she sounded now almost like a missionary reading the Bible to a happily naked

16

heathen. She went on reverently for a few more sentences, and at the first pause I broke in.

"The All-High, I take it, is Trammel?"

"Mr. Trammel, of course."

Of course. I knew already that Trammel held some kind of nightly confessional, but this was the first mention of any Healing Room—and the first time I'd heard him called the All-High. A few others had spoken of the bum as the Master, however. He was in solid with his flock.

I asked Mary, "What kind of advice or help could Felicity have needed from—from the All-High?"

"I don't know. She didn't say anything to me."

I got up, thanked them, and left. Mrs. Lewis said goodby, which was the only thing she'd said to me after hello. She'd kept a very beady eye on me, though, while I talked to her daughter.

I made a few more fast calls, then rang the bell where one Betha Green lived. Betha was a surprise. It had got so I could anticipate what Trammelites would look like and how they'd be dressed. So far they'd all been so drab in appearance, somber, sad-looking, that you'd think the Master had just kicked the bucket.

Betha Green, though, looked pretty good. She wore an orange sweater that, for a Trammelite, was a sin, plus a pair of brown slacks, and was barefoot. I guessed she was seventeen or eighteen, and she wasn't a bad-looking gal.

When I introduced myself and told her I wanted to talk about Felicity, she smiled and said, "How is she? I haven't seen her for a couple of weeks. Ashamed of myself, really." She sat in a wooden chair on the porch and motioned me to another.

"I was hoping you had seen her," I said. "She left her house sometime last night. Hasn't been back."

Surprise grew into shock on her face. "Are you serious?" I nodded and Betha said anxiously, "Oh, I hope she isn't hurt."

"I haven't any idea where she is or what's happened. That's what I'm trying to find out. I hoped you might give me some help."

"How funny! I wish I could help. I really do."

The conversation finally came around to Trammelism and I said, "I understand that the All-High has a Healing Room where—"

She laughed in an odd way. "You mean Trammel?"

"Yeah." This one was really a surprise. I'd even fallen

17

into the habit of referring to the boss as the All-High myself; when I didn't, or neglected the "Mr." before his name, terrible things happened to Trammelite faces. I said, still being careful, "Everyone calls him either that or the Master, so—"

"Oh, that's a lot of baloney."

"Balo— Aren't you a Trammelite, Miss Green?"

"I used to be, but I stopped going. I got tired of it."

"Oh?" I thought she might go on, and I tried to get more out of her on that subject, but she had dropped it. I said, "You know Felicity pretty well, don't you?"

"Uh-huh. We've been friends for years. I haven't seen her so much the last few months, but that's just because I stopped going to meetings."

"Can you think of any reason at all why she might have run away from home?"

"Uh-uh. I don't think she'd run away, though," she said quietly. "It just wouldn't be like her, no matter what."

"How do you mean?"

"You'd have to know her. That would hurt her mother, and she wouldn't hurt anybody for a million dollars."

"Funny, though. She must have left her room by herself. No telling what might have happened to her then, but leaving the house must have been her own idea."

"I just can't believe it."

"That reminds me." I told her about last night's call and Betha said she hadn't phoned. "She wrote down the name Dixon. Nobody seems—"

I stopped. We were both sitting in the wooden chairs and Betha had one hand resting on the edge of the seat, fingers curled loosely around it. She was looking toward the street, so only part of her profile was visible, but her hand gripped the seat convulsively. Her knuckles turned white.

She didn't turn her head or speak, so I said, "What does that name mean to you?"

"Nothing. Should it?" Her voice was controlled, but her hand was still squeezed tight against the wood.

"Look at me a minute."

She turned toward me. Her face seemed a little paler, but otherwise she appeared normal, the same as before. I said, "That sort of jarred you, didn't it?"

She smiled and her hand relaxed. "What do you mean?"

"When I said Dixon. You got all wound up."

She laughed. "That's silly. I don't know what you mean."

18

That was her story and she stuck to it for the rest of our conversation. Maybe I was wrong; I didn't think so. I got up and said, "Thanks. If you think of anything that might help me—help Felicity, that is—call me, huh? I'm in the book."

"I will. Honestly, I will."

Arthur Trammel's stamping grounds, where he stamped out sin, were several miles north of L.A., almost to the town of Raleigh. I headed north. For the first time in my life, I was looking forward to seeing Trammel. I'd now talked to everybody on my list, all the routine was done, and from here on in my search for Felicity would boil down to tedious legwork, or waiting to see if one of the lines I'd put out paid off—unless Trammel could give me some kind of lead.

There seemed a pretty good chance that he might be able to. During the morning I'd been talking almost exclusively to his followers. Careful as I'd been to try sounding neutral when I spoke of him, my contempt must have coated my voice a few times, and I consequently got several very dirty looks. I now knew for sure that Arthur Trammel, to his flock, was hallelujah in three dimensions, about sixteen feet tall, and each inch irresistible. He was the Trammelites' friend, father, confidant, and wailing wall, a kind of cross between the father confessor and amateur psychoanalyst. The concensus had been that if anybody could help me, it would be the All-High. I hoped that was true. Mary Lewis had told me Felicity had gone to Trammel's confessional. And I figured that if Felicity had been in any kind of trouble, been worried or upset, she might have confided in Trammel or asked his help, as so many others had. It didn't seem likely that she'd have gone to her mother.

I drove onto the Trammelite grounds about noon. Ordinarily Trammel might have been difficult to locate, since he was often making speeches, meeting with committees, drawing up resolutions, and so on. But every Sunday noon he met here at headquarters with the other Guardians and they all spent an hour or so figuring out how to save the world from flaming hell. I parked my Cad in a big lot with three other Cads, a Packard, and a Buick, thinking that if the prospect of looking upon Trammel alone was unpalatable, all seven Guardians at once would be unhealthy.

Of the group I'd met only Trammel, but I knew the

19

names and appearances of the others from their frequent pictures and pronunciamentos in the local press. Those pronunciamentos made it clear that all seven felt that the difference between men and women should be a secret. Their current campaign—there was always a current campaign—was plastered over the papers and was directed, as usual, against what they called "filth." To me it was merely further proof that the Guardians wanted a return to those good old days when women covered up everything except their instincts; it was, basically, a frantic protest against "cleavage."

The Guardians would be meeting in the tent, but since this was my first visit to Trammelism's center, I looked around before getting out of the Cad. This was a pleasant location, surrounded by trees growing on low hills. The tent itself, as big as a Ringling Brothers job, was ahead of me and on my right. Directly behind it was a small cliff, rising only slightly higher than the tent's top, and a big cave was being blasted and dug into its face. Work had been in progress for the last month and a half-dozen men were back there now around a puffing steam shovel. This operation, the Guardians declared, was destined to become Trammelism's "Eternal House." From the cliff's solid rock would be blasted a big room, in which Arthur Trammel would hold forth on special occasions, and which would "last through the ages." I told you they were crazy.

A fit's throw beyond the cliff and farther left, almost directly opposite my Cad, was a low, black building called the Truth Room. A few yards farther away was a small frame house where Trammel himself lived. I got out of the car and walked on green grass beneath flowing pepper trees to the tent. It was gloomy inside, but at the far end a light was burning, illuminating a wide raised platform or stage on which, at night, Trammel would stand and speak. On stage now was a big rectangular table around which the seven Guardians were grouped. Walking down one of the two aisles between rows of wooden seats I could hear Trammel's melodious, beautifully modulated voice, a surprisingly lovely voice for so unlovely a bastard.

When I got closer I noticed that an outsider was present, since eight people were seated around the table. Trammel was standing, addressing the others—until I walked up on the stage and he saw me.

20

He was saying, ". . . as our survey has indicated. There-fore, I am sure we all agree that it is our duty, yes, our—*Sheldon Scott!*"

"Good morning, Mr. Trammel. Sorry to burst in, but I need some information."

"What are *you* doing here, you—"

"If you've got a minute, I'd appreciate a little help. It's important." While he glared at me, taking his time about answering, I noticed that he was still nauseating in appearance.

There was no doubt about it, only one Trammel ex-isted in all the world. It wasn't just his ugliness that set him apart from other men, but his particular ugliness. It was almost as though you were looking not at his face but at what he was thinking. Just under six feet tall, spike-thin, with small round eyes that seemed perpetually wid-ened in surprise under monstrously bushy black brows, and dressed always in black, he looked like an undertaker who had embalmed himself by mistake.

Trammel's head was so freakishly thin that his brain must have looked like a waffle, and wisps of graying hair rested on white scalp that looked like bone. In the narrow space between those dark eyes protruded a long, curved, grappling-hook nose.

He was staring at me the same way he had on that day when I'd kicked him out of my office. Finally he said, "You know better than to come here, Scott. And as for any help—"

"Wait a minute. I'm not after help for me personally; this is about a Trammelite, one of your followers."

The icy look remained another second, then slowly he smiled. That was the unkindest cut of all. It was as if in-visible hooks pulled one lip up and the other down, the smile of a bald-headed man who had just been bombed by an eagle. "One of my followers?" he said. "Ah, well . . . I am always anxious to help any of my children."

"I'm trying to find a girl. Felicity Gifford. She's been missing a couple of days and may be in trouble, or hurt. Maybe she's just run away from home. Anyway, nobody seems to know what happened to her, and I thought she might have talked to you—or one of the other Guardians."

I glanced around at them. The two men beside Tram-mel were a retired doctor and a practicing mortician. The four others were called women: Andrews, a lady lawyer

21

with a small mustache; two maiden ladies, each of whom looked several hundred years old; and the shriveled president of an all-female temperance society that demanded temperance in everything except temperance societies. The extra guy I'd noticed, the outsider, was a man who seemed familiar in appearance. I couldn't place him, but knew I'd seen him before.

"Felicity Gifford?" Trammel said. "I can't quite—"

"She's young, sixteen. Everybody I've talked to seems to think she's tops. Sings in your choral group."

"Oh, yes. Felicity." He nodded. "One of our finest children. I recall her now, of course, but I haven't spoken to her for weeks. I'm sorry, I do wish I could help. I am always ready to extend a helping hand—"

I interrupted, knowing I couldn't last through one of his sanctimonious speeches. "The thing is, I've talked with several Trammelites who told me you often help them with their problems, advise them. One said Felicity attended your confession a week or so back. That figures, if she was fouled up in any way, and I hoped she might have told you if anything was worrying her."

"Perhaps," Trammel said coldly, "but I never know to whom I speak. Anonymity is strictly preserved. I'm afraid none of us can be of help." He glanced around the table and the others shook their heads.

That seemed to wrap it up, and I was more disappointed than I'd thought I would be. I guess I'd been hoping irrationally that here I'd get some kind of lead to Felicity, and now I was right back where I'd started. The only thing worth remembering from the whole morning was the way Betha Green had acted, grabbing her chair and, I felt sure, lying to me.

I looked at Trammel. "One other thing. Does the name Dixon mean anything to you?"

He blinked at me. "What?"

"Dixon. Probably it's somebody's name. I thought it might be a Trammelite. Conceivably it's a lead to Felicity."

Trammel said, "It means nothing to me." Nobody at the table reacted in any way. The extra guy, I noticed, had a small notebook open before him and was jotting something in it. I almost had him made, but then I became aware of Trammel sputtering beside me.

". . . so get out. We cannot offer you any assistance, and I listened to you only because I hoped to help one of

22

my friends. If we should learn anything of Felicity—or others in distress, for that matter—we would hardly inform a man of your stripe, Scott."

I looked back at him. "Huh? What stripe are you—"

He rode right over me. Either Trammel was finally getting back at me for my attitude the other time we'd met, or he was purposely trying to make me mad. He was succeeding in making me mad. When he spouted, "There are too many decent people—" I cut him off.

"Stow it, mister. Get this through your head: I don't give a damn what your opinion of me is. I'm only interested in the girl. Otherwise I wouldn't have come within a mile of here. Felicity's a young, sweet kid, and pretty enough, and I hate to think what might—"

Trammel's small eyes lit up and he said huskily, "I know what you think. I know your kind, Scott. She *is* young and pretty, isn't she? I know why you're interested in her. Of course you want to find her."

"Why, you emaciated buzzard." That—even from Trammel—had knocked me for a loop. I was so stunned I let him keep on yakking.

"You'll get no help from us. And I demand that you never come here again."

"Listen, mister, don't start demanding anything."

He was almost shouting. "I further demand that you stay away from my Trammelite friends and associates! I'll not have you bothering them, talking to them, annoying them. They are fine, decent men and women, and I'll not permit a man of your disgusting morals and filthy thoughts—"

"You slimy bastard," I said, and he stopped in midsentence. I leaned forward with my hands on the table and stared at Trammel as he shrank back. "One more crack out of you," I said softly, "and you'll have teeth in your stomach. I've had all of you I can take. What the hell's the matter with you, mister? You got an old war wound or something?"

He started to sputter again, but I kept going. "Filthy, huh? I guess everything's filthy to you except the nice dirty money those ignorant Trammelites of yours toss in the kitty. You and your goddamned pea-brained guardians of everything. What's today's meeting about? Somebody say a dirty word?"

It was an effort, but I forced myself to shut my big mouth. Anything else I might have said would have been

23

no more effective or clever than my last remarks.

The other Guardians were standing now, faces livid, arms waving. Only the extra guy was still seated, and he was grinning almost happily at me, apparently enjoying himself. The others weren't.

Trammel was still sputtering. A short stocky guy with a face like ham and eggs, big eyes yellowish in a pink face, was literally jumping up and down. Andrews of the small mustache was waggling a bony finger and crying, "It's men like you who make the rest of us bear the cross of your sins!"

I let her run down, then turned to go. Trammel shouted, "Just a minute! You animal, we'll not permit—"

"Oh, shut up." I'd intended to leave quietly, but I swung around to face him. "Quit telling me what you'll permit and what you demand, Trammel."

"You've not heard the last of this!"

"Since you mention it, you haven't either. I'll ride the bunch of you to death if I get half a chance."

Then it was quiet; nobody was speaking or even gasping. The familiar face of the other man still wore his grin. I turned and walked down from the platform.

As I started toward the tent's exit, Trammel called in a strangled voice, "You've made a grave mistake, speaking to us like this, Scott."

I kept walking but looked over my shoulder. "Sure. Incidentally, you ever find your pornographic library, Trammel?"

He didn't tell me, and I went on out.

Chapter Four

I WAS SHOWERING when the chimes bonged, so I wrapped a towel around my middle, picked up a bourbon-and-water highball sitting on the washbasin, and dripped toward the front door.

It was after seven P.M. now, but the burn Trammel and his Guardians had built in me hadn't yet died completely. Since noon I'd talked to a few dozen more people, made about fifty phone calls, driven over half the town

—all without getting a single lead to Felicity. The checking had kept me busy, but now that I'd had time to relax a bit, both my gripe with Trammel and my worry about Felicity were growing.

I couldn't understand how the girl could have disappeared so completely, and the more time that passed without a trace of her, the more worried I'd become. I figured she was the type to flip good if she flipped. In my job I'd seen plenty of cases about like hers, young kids, held in all their lives and kept ignorant of their own and others' emotions, who didn't know how to handle those emotions when they were brand-new and just starting to work inside them. Most of them got hurt, some of them badly hurt, simply because they didn't know what the score was.

But those were my last thoughts of either Felicity or Trammel for a few minutes. The chimes bonged again and I opened the door and I thought: Wow!

It was a woman, a doll, a sensational tomato who looked as if she'd just turned twenty-one, but had obviously signaled for the turn a long time ago. She was tall, and lovely all over, maybe five-seven, and she wore a V-necked white blouse as if she were the gal who'd invented cleavage just for fun.

I gawked, and she smiled with plump red lips, beautiful lips that undoubtedly had said yes much more often than no, and I said, "Come in, come in, hello. Hello, miss. Miss?"

"Miss Perrine." She brought the faint scent of perfume in with her. Her hair was short and blonde, and her voice was a soft huskiness saying, as I shut the door and turned around, "My goodness, letting a girl in when you're dressed like that. Undressed."

"I didn't plan it, it—"

"Just a towel. You think you're making an impression? Well, you are. *Goodness*, you're big."

She rattled that off, smiling a yes-*yes* smile and blinking big green eyes at me. After a false start I said, "Ah . . . sit down. I was taking a shower. In the shower. Very clean fellow, clean-cut, clean. . . . Can I get something . . . get *you* something? A drink? Cigarette? Food?"

She walked from me toward my oversized black divan and I noticed she wore a blue skirt that she also filled admirably.

"Excuse me," I said. "Won't be a minute."

I was a whirlwind in the bedroom and came back wearing cordovans, tan slacks, and a vivid red sports shirt. She was looking at my two tanks of tropical fish, one with guppies in it, the other containing a pair of neons I was trying to spawn. The guppies were sinning; the little devils are always sinning.

"Hello," I said. "Here I am. Here . . . we are."

Peering at the fish, she said, "What are these?"

"Neon tetras." She was puzzled by a square of glass hanging outside the tank, so I explained. "That's a one-way mirror. I'm trying to spawn them, and neons are tricky, don't like to be disturbed while spawning. Who does? Ha. I can peek through the mirror and see if they lay any eggs, and they can't see me, don't even know I'm out here. Good?"

She batted long lashes. "Peeking at them. How awful. You *are* Shell Scott, aren't you?"

"Yes, ma'am. Detective. Fish fancier. Bachelor."

"Just so you're the detective." She stopped smiling and said, "I phoned but your line was busy, so I came over. I think maybe I can help you."

"You most certainly—"

"Unless you've already found the girl."

That stopped me cold. "What girl?"

"Felicity Gifford. You are looking for her, aren't you?"

"Yeah. How did you know?"

"It's in the paper, right on the front page. I just read it. That's why I called. I really—"

"Do you know where she is? Have you seen her?"

She shook her head. "I've never even met her. I just started to say I really don't know anything for sure. Actually, I feel a little silly now that I'm here."

"Look, if you know anything at all, spit it out. I mean, tell me. No matter what it is, it's more than I've got now."

Her name was Jo, Miss Jo Perrine, and she lived here in Hollywood with her mother and her mother's brother, a rich, eccentric egg named Randolph Hunt. Her uncle wasn't a Trammelite, but he had several times gone to their tent meetings and had met Felicity. He knew her fairly well and, like almost everybody else, thought she was a little doll. An hour or so earlier this evening Jo and her uncle, Mr. Hunt, had been in the front room; he'd been reading the newspapers, noticed Felicity's name, and mentioned it to Jo, expressing surprise and the hope that she was all right. He'd finished the story, mumbled a

26

couple of things Jo hadn't caught, and then suddenly left.

"It was funny, I guess," Jo said to me, "but I didn't think anything about it then. Later I read the story myself, and when I saw Miss Dixon's name down near the end, I started to wonder about—"

"Who? Miss Dixon?"

"Yes. That is, I saw the name Dixon. Uncle knows a woman named Dixon, and with her name and Felicity's and the Trammelites and all in the story, it made me wonder if it could have anything to do with Uncle. Besides, I thought it might be something you'd want to know."

I stood up. "You bet it is. Where can I find this Dixon?"

"I don't know, Mr. Scott. I don't know where she lives. But if it is the woman you were talking about, I thought you might find her through Uncle." She frowned and added, "I haven't even any idea where he'd be now, though."

I sat down again. The name Felicity had written on that pad might not have any connection with the woman Hunt knew, and even if they were the same, it didn't help me much. There are 258 people named Dixon listed in the L.A. phone book; that was one of the angles the two guys I'd hired were laboriously checking.

Most of the steam went out of me, because even with this info I still didn't know what the hell I could do. I asked Jo to phone her home and see if Hunt were there, but her call drew a blank, as did our next few minutes of conversation.

Finally I thought of something that should have puzzled me earlier: How this stuff had got into the papers at all. I asked Jo and she said, "I don't know, but there's a big story. I brought my paper up with me."

"Swell. As long as I'm just sitting here, I might as well read the thing."

She reached to the divan beside her and picked up a folded copy of the *Ledger*, then leaned forward, way forward, and handed it to me.

I took the paper, flipped it open—and immediately understood several things: how and why the story had been written, who the grinning stranger at the Guardian meeting had been, and that the war on Shell Scott had been declared—and not only Guardians were attacking.

The stuff about me occupied the two left-hand columns on the front page under a head reading: "Detective At-

tacks Arthur Trammel." A subhead beneath it declared:
"Shell Scott Threatens Guardians. Calls Church-goers Ignorant." It was by-lined Ira Borch—the grinning stranger,
a slimy sonofabitch who'd been on my can for six months.
A little too late, I'd finally placed him. Before I read a
word of the story, I knew what to expect. I also knew I'd
have more trouble with these guys, all of them; this was
just the beginning.

Trammel had plenty of reason to hate my guts; but
Borch and his rag had even more. The *Ledger* is an L.A.
newspaper so far to the left that it might as well be pub-
lished in Moscow, and Ira Borch is a new-definition lib-
eral. For half a year I'd been high on their smear list.
Six months back I'd been investigating a Communist-
dominated union and had been forced, in self-defense,
to shoot an alleged Commie in his alleged brain. It had
killed him, too, since in that particular instance the Fifth
Amendment hadn't been any protection for him. My story
of the justifiable homicide stood up, the alleged Commie,
as usual, refusing to answer any questions at all, so after
the coroner's inquest I was in the clear as far as the law
was concerned.

You'd have thought, however, that I had set fire to
the *Ledger* building and the editor's pants. You would
have thought I'd pooped Khrushchev. The *Ledger* had
made a big thing out of it, not quite calling the homicide
cold-blooded murder, and since then had laid it on me
whenever it got a chance.

It laid it on today. There was only brief mention of
my "allegedly" looking for Felicity Gifford, and near the
story's end was a single sentence about my having said
one "Dixon" might be a lead to her; mainly the story con-
sisted of a Borch-style résumé of my previous crimes, including the killing of a persecuted union official, plus
seven quotes, one from each Guardian. Apparently the
Guardians were agreed I might be the devil himself, come
up here to give them hell. The story wound up in a blaze
of babble about my "obscene language, threats of physical
violence, and condemnation of the church."

I said to Jo, "You'd never know from reading this that
I was talking about Trammel's cult, and called the Trammelites ignorant. If those characters are churchgoers, I'm
the angel Gabriel."

"You don't have to explain to me, Mr. Scott." She
smiled. "One of the reasons I came up here is because it

28

was the Ledger that carried the story. None of the other papers did."

"I take it you don't have much use for the sheet, either."

"None, Mr. Scott."

"Baby," I said, "call me Shell. And if you ever need a detective for anything, I'm at your service."

She smiled. "For anything?"

"For anything at . . . Well."

She chuckled and said, "Oh, what would I need a detective's service for, anyway?" and the chuckle turned into a throaty laugh.

When she quieted down I said, "Jo, I'd love to mix highballs and carry on like mad here, but I'm itchy. There must be some way to find Mr. Hunt. Where does he usually go? Doesn't he have some kind of hangout where I could look for him?"

"There's no telling where he'd be. Probably with one of his girl friends. That's about all he does. He doesn't have any vices like drinking or smoking, just women."

"That's a vice? If I have to, I'll go knock on all his girl friends' doors. Give me some names and I'll start. Maybe one of them would know where he is, or even know this Dixon. Incidentally, you ever see her? Know what she looks like?"

Jo nodded. "She came out to the house once. About forty-something, fairly thin, big black mole on her cheek. That's about all I can remember." She pinched her chin, brows furrowed. "There's a woman named Olive Fair-weather that Uncle's been seeing a lot of lately. And I just remembered he said something this morning about having a date tonight. I don't know who with."

"Think he might have gone to her place?"

"Maybe. The mushy way they act, they must like each other. I saw them together at the house once and they kept beaming at each other, winking and gurgling. He calls her Lover-gal, of all things. She's in her forties and he's fifty-four, but they act like teen-agers. I think she even calls him Lover-boy when nobody else is around. Isn't that silly?"

"Not if it makes them happy. You know where she lives?"

She didn't, so I got out my phone book and city directory. While flipping the pages, I asked her what Hunt looked like, and she said, "About six feet, and he's pretty strong. He'll have real colorful clothes on. He's sort of

. . . odd. Oh, and he's bald. Not bald—I mean the other day he shaved all his hair off."

I looked up at her. "He did, huh? Well, that is a little odd." The phone book didn't help, but an Olive Fairweather was listed in the directory. I got up, grabbed a coat and my gun, just in case, then took Jo down to her car and got my Cad rolling.

There was a dim light on in the front room of Olive Fairweather's house. I walked to the entrance and rang the bell. The screen door was unlocked, the inside door standing open, and almost as soon as I pressed the buzzer a squeaky voice from inside called, "Come i-in."

I said, "This is—"

"Come in, come in."

"But—"

"Come in, come in, hurry *up!*"

I went in. It was a mistake.

The light was dim, but not dim enough. Reclining on a couch was a gal who missed complete nudity only because of a strategically draped Mexican serape, and now I knew what they meant when they said, "Sex rears its ugly head." Her eyes were rolled toward the ceiling, either in dreamy ecstasy or in a spasm, and even with no clothes on she had a plunging neckline.

"I knew you'd come, Lover-boy," she cooed. "I knew you would."

"Lady," I said, "you're in for a hell of a shock. I am not Lover-boy."

Chapter Five

THERE WAS A SQUAWK and a flurry and a blur of Olive and her serape. She loped out of sight, and I thought: Hunt isn't eccentric; he's crazy.

Olive Fairweather came back wearing a green robe and low-heeled shoes. When she turned on the overhead lights I got a good look at her. She had short mouse-brown hair, rather nice full lips, and gray eyes. But they weren't pretty gray eyes. Not dawn gray, slate gray, or even muddy gray. They were a sort of Dorian gray. I told her my name and that I was looking for Hunt.

"I thought Randy—Mr. Hunt—was—would be here," she said. "I'm sorry. I mean, I shouldn't have . . ."

"It's all right. I shouldn't have busted in. You were expecting Mr. Hunt?"

"Yes, half an hour ago." She sat down on the couch. "I don't know what's the matter. He promised he'd come."

"I'm anxious to find him, Miss Fairweather." I told her I was looking for Felicity Gifford, had reason to believe Hunt might have information that would help me, and added, "I understand he knows a woman named Dixon."

She straightened up on the couch so fast she almost came off it. "Miss Dixon!" she yelped. "Why, the old goat! He's gone out to Greenhaven to see *her*. Why, the old . . . the old *goat!*"

Just like that, bull's-eye, I thought. "Greenhaven, huh? Where is the place? What's Dixon's first name?" And Olive Fairweather suddenly clammed.

There was a funny look on her face and she calmed down in a hurry. One hand was pressed against her throat as she said slowly, "Oh, I . . . That was just a guess. It doesn't mean anything. I was being foolish."

"Miss Fairweather, it's important. That's exactly what I've been trying to find out. What's this Greenhaven?"

She licked her lips. "It's just a man's home. Mr. Greenhaven. A . . . friend of Mr. Hunt's."

"Mr. Greenhaven?"

"Well, it's—it's Mr. Green. His home. Immensely wealthy. He calls it Greenhaven."

She was a lousy liar. More credit to her, because the lousy liars don't practice much, but that didn't help me. And she kept on not helping me. I explained about Felicity and why anything Olive could tell me was important, went from persuasive to volubly griped, but it was no good; she had no more to say. Finally I got up and headed for the door.

She came after me and said, "If you should see him anywhere, please tell him I'm . . . worried. Nobody else ever comes to see me, and he said he'd be here. I hope nothing's happened."

"Yeah," I said, "you're worried. So are Mrs. Gifford and a lot of other people. So am I. Maybe so is Felicity."

She opened her mouth, then closed it firmly.

31

"O.K., lady," I said, "I'll tell him if I get the chance." I drove away, not quite so angry with her as I might have been, because of that one thing she'd said: "Nobody else ever comes to see me."

Greenhaven was a high cement wall and a big iron gate. At least, that was all I could see of it. I had found a flock of Greens in the phone book, plus one Greenhaven, the address here, and six telephone numbers.

I parked off the narrow street near the wall, went to the gate, and banged on it. A guy walked over from my right somewhere and peered out at me. "What you want?"

His chops hung three or four inches above mine, so I glanced down to see what he was standing on. Just enormous feet; he was a monster. That, plus the way Olive had acted, made me unsure of how to handle this. I said, "Does a guy named Green own this place?"

"Don't get lippy. Who you want to see?"

"Well . . . Miss Dixon. There's a Miss Dixon here, isn't there?"

"Yeah." He pulled out a big key and unlocked the gate. I followed him to a small shedlike room, where he scribbled the time, my name, and Miss Dixon's on a pad, tore off the top sheet, and handed it to me. I turned around and got my first good look at Greenhaven. Approximately half an acre of lawn extended up to a large gray building at the end of a graveled drive, and fifty or more people were in sight at tables and chairs, or sitting on the lawn. There were lights burning all over the place.

"Having a party, huh?" I said.

"Yeah, party. Don't get lippy."

"Who's getting—" I let it go, walked up the drive. Looked like a party, all right. Big one. There were a lot of elderly cats doddering about, also a number of younger men and women. As I passed a table where two middle-aged women were seated carrying on a quiet conversation, I got my first inkling that something was out of joint in this joint.

One of the women was saying, "How do you like this dress, Mattie? Don't you think it looks nice?"

"No, I don't. It makes you look like an old hag."

"Oh, how silly. It can't be that bad."

"Haw!"

"Oh, Mattie. Isn't that a little strong?"

"Not strong enough. Makes you look like an old hag."

"Oh, dear. I thought it did something for me."

"Does. Makes you look like an old hag."

Then I was out of earshot. I wanted to go back and listen some more. I knew both those people had been women, and therefore I couldn't have heard what I thought I'd heard. That was a shock, but the next thing I saw stunned me—for an entirely different reason.

From the corner of my eye I noticed a woman dressed in white looking toward me. I glanced at her and stopped dead in my tracks. She was *everything* I like. A little dish who could make me forget I had ever seen Miss Perrine. She had big dark eyes, one brow raised above the other as she looked at me, a saucy little nose, and red lips that pouted just enough. And she had red hair. Hair like women used to have before they started masquerading as men, long and thick and glossy, brushing her shoulders. But that wasn't all; she had a shape that, even motionless, was nearly as sensational as Lilly Christine doing calisthenics.

I might have stood there gawking indefinitely except that I heard a bunch of yowls and yells behind me and looked over my shoulder at something so peculiar that I kept staring. Fifty feet away was a guy playing badminton; at least, that's what it looked like, except there wasn't any net or racket or shuttlecock. No partner, either, and for a moment I thought maybe he was doing ballet exercises.

He was certainly swatting away energetically enough, rushing forward and back and leaping into the air. He threw something invisible down to the grass, then ran toward me and leaped over the net. Can't be badminton, must be tennis, I thought. And then I began wondering just what the hell was going on out here.

The energetic guy was still running straight at me, but about five yards away he skidded to a stop, bobbed his head at me, and grinned. "Throw me the ball," he said.

"Huh? What . . . what ball?"

"The ball, the ball! Throw me my ball!"

For a couple of seconds I actually looked around for it, then swallowed. The realization had suddenly hit me that I was in some kind of cackle factory—and at the same moment I understood why such a big ape had been out at the gate. Probably several more apes were handy in case of uprisings. The tennis player was raising a hell of a racket, and because I wanted no uprisings now that I

33

seemed close to Miss Dixon, I said, "Sure, fellow, don't get excited. Where—uh, where's the ball?"

"Right there." He pointed at my feet.

Feeling very damned silly, I said, "Oh, that ball," bent over, and pawed at the ground. "Not there, you fool," the guy shouted at the top of his lungs. "By the other foot. You blind or something?"

I grabbed some air by the other foot, straightened up, and threw it to him. He beamed, leaped into the air, and caught it, then ran off without so much as a thank you.

The little red-haired gal was still watching me, frowning now, and I opened my mouth to say something, then closed it. I couldn't think of anything that would make sense of this. Finally I decided to play it light. I laughed and said, "Can't see a thing without my glasses." She wasn't amused. So I walked on up to the gray building, through a big door like the entrance to a library, and into a short high-ceilinged corridor with a polished dark floor. Two closed doors with plain frosted-glass windows were on my right. I walked to the corridor's end, where it bisected another long hallway lined with more doors. Just around the corner was a room with a wire screen enclosing it. Inside were rows of wooden compartments and I could see clothing, boxes, packages in them.

The only person in sight was a small, slightly potbellied man walking down the hall toward me. He was about fifty years old, dressed in a brown suit, and whistling silently through pursed lips. The little man stopped alongside me. "Good evening," he said. "I haven't seen you before, have I?"

"Evening. I just got here."

"May I be of assistance?"

"Maybe. I'm looking for Miss Dixon—or a man named Randolph Hunt, if he's here."

He pursed his lips. "Nurse Dixon, eh? She won't be back for"—he glanced at his wrist watch—"several days."

"She's a nurse, huh? She . . Several days?"

He pursed his lips again. "Yes." He was silent for a few seconds, then said, "Perhaps I can help you. I am Dr. Nichols, the chief psychiatrist."

That settled it. "Doctor," I said, "where am I?"

"Don't you know, my boy?"

"I mean I know this is Greenhaven, but what is it?"

"Why, Greenhaven—" He broke off, staring over my shoulder. "Oh, dear," he said.

34

I looked around, and there was the little beauty with the hair and shape and everything. She was standing about a yard away, looking at me. "What's the matter?"

The doctor didn't speak, so I said, "I was just explaining to Dr. Nichols here that I've got—"

She interrupted. "Just a moment. *I'm* Dr. Nichols."

"Yeah, sure," I said. "We're all *three* Dr. Nichols." I was starting to get a little griped, because finding out anything in this place was beginning to stack up like a lifetime job, and I was in a hurry.

The girl said quietly, "I am Dr. Lynette Nichols. Follow me, please."

I went along. We all walked down the hall to a door marked, "Dr. Nichols, Chief Psychiatrist." She opened the door and said to me, "I have to take Mr. Wallace to his room, but I'll talk to you in a minute. What's your name?"

She spoke crisply, and I noticed that what I'd earlier thought was a white dress was actually a starched uniform. "Shell Scott," I said. "I'm a private detective."

Her lips curved upward a little at the corners. "What's so funny?" I asked her. "Look, I need some help, some information—from *somebody* here—and it's important." I told her why I was at Greenhaven and what I wanted to know.

She nodded. "All right, I'll be back in a minute."

"Please hurry, will you? I wasn't kidding when I said it was important."

She nodded again, turned, and went out, the guy following her docilely. I stood in the doorway and watched her walk down the hall. She paused for a moment and spoke with two white-jacketed men, whom I assumed were either doctors or a couple of Napoleons, and all three looked back toward me. She went on down the corridor. The two men walked up to me.

One of them, a big-nosed guy wearing rimless glasses, introduced himself as Dr. Wolfe, and the other guy as Yancey. Yancey was a thin, pale egg with washed-out blue eyes. Wolfe asked my name, and after I told him he said softly, "I understand you're looking for happiness, Mr. Scott. Well, we all are—"

"What the hell are you talking about?" Man, you couldn't tell the nuts from the squirrels in here. "What do you mean, I'm looking . . . Oh, Felicity," I jerked my head down the hall. "That what she told you?" He nod-

35

ded. "It's a girl's name," I said. "Felicity Gifford. And I wish to God everybody here would stop giving me this fancy runaround. Tell me something. Is that little doll really a psychiatrist?"

Wolfe nodded, light bouncing from his glasses. "Yes, Lyn Nichols. She's the chief psychiatrist here." He turned suddenly and left with the other man.

I perched on the desk and looked around at filing cabinets, a small table, and some chairs, wondering if everybody were goofy in this place, then got up and paced back and forth nervously. After a while I heard footsteps and glanced at my watch, thinking the girl was returning; it was already nine-twenty. A guy came inside, though, the big ape from the gate. Right behind him was another monster. The first guy walked toward me, said, "Mr. Scott, wasn't it?" and stuck out his hand.

I extended my arm and said, "That's right—"

The words ended in a grunt, because the guy latched onto my wrist and jerked me toward him. Even in here it was the last thing I'd expected, and I was off balance. As I stumbled half a step toward him, he reached behind me and grabbed the left shoulder of my coat, spun me as easily as if I'd weighed ten pounds, twisting my arm behind me. I started to jerk away too late.

He was fast, and he was good. Undoubtedly he got a lot of practice with this sort of thing in Greenhaven, but there was one thing he probably didn't know: I'd had a lot more unarmed defense in the Marines, and judo elsewhere, and plain rough-and-tumble all over, than he could have guessed.

"Watch it, mister," I said. "What's the idea?"

"Come along quiet," he said. "Be easier on you."

He wasn't even breathing hard, and he sounded almost bored. The other guy stood in front of me and a little to the side in case he was needed. I still wanted to know what was coming off.

"Listen, stupid, I'm not a patient," I said. "So unwind your—" and that was all.

He jerked my arm up behind my back and shoved me forward, and it hurt enough so that I no longer cared to reason with the bastard. He had me in a good arm lock, and he must have expected me to be awed and co-operative. I was neither. I let him shove me almost to the door, then I stepped straight up instead of ahead and slammed my heel down on his instep as hard as I could. The thin

36

bones crumpled like paper. As he yelled and loosened his grip I jerked my arm free, swung toward him with my left fist on its way. It landed with a satisfying smack against his lips.

He staggered back. I stepped aside, ducking, as the other guy hit me from behind and bounced past me. When he spun toward me raising a hamlike fist, he was wide open, and because it was his left fist moving, I swung my open right hand down first, cracked its edge against his collarbone. It caved in with a sound like that of bone breaking, which is exactly what it was, and he yelled just before the edge of my left palm landed and broke his collarbone on the other side.

The guy who'd grabbed me in the first place was facing me, his face dripping red, but he didn't worry me much now because the other guy wouldn't be lifting even a finger for a while. And that was where I made my mistake—assuming there were only two of them.

My back was to the door and I heard the small sound behind me, but the sound immediately after that was a great big crashing sound, and it was inside my head. I was conscious clear down to the floor, even felt myself sprawling out on the carpet, but that was all, and it got black everywhere.

I couldn't have been out very long. When I came to a couple of guys were carrying me down the corridor. Both guys were strangers; the other two apes wouldn't be carrying anything but grudges for a long time. It took me a little while, but I figured out that I was on a stretcher and in a strait jacket. Everything was blurred, but I could see the two doctors and the little psychiatrist, or whatever the hell they were.

I started talking softly, but I soon was yelling. They all ignored me. I kept yelling; they kept carrying me down the corridor.

Chapter Six

I REALIZED my eyes were closed and forced them wide again. I'd lost track of the number of times that had happened; with the drug making my thoughts sluggish, my body numb, it was difficult to know if my eyes were actually open or not. I couldn't even think any more. I'd gone back over this whole day without remembering a thing to explain what had happened, explain why somebody had tried to kill me—and I never would know unless I got out of here.

I arched my body violently, more in anger than with any purpose, felt pain burn across my back, but pushed with all my strength at the cloth around me—and heard the sound of canvas tearing. My arms moved. The shock of that movement, plus the sharp pain, cleared my head a little, and I understood what had happened. The blade that had cut me must first have sliced nearly through the canvas sleeves that held my arms and extended on around my body; my sudden movement had torn them the rest of the way.

In another few seconds, my hands were bare; soon I'd pulled the jacket off and was standing beside the bed, sweat beaded on my face. Dizziness swept over me and I almost fell, catching the bed's edge for support; then I groped my way to the room's rear, forced the window up, slid through, and dropped to the ground outside. My coat and gun had been taken from me before I'd been put in the strait jacket, and it was cold; fog had drifted inland from the sea. For a moment I leaned back against the building's wall. Felicity's name spun in my brain. I knew that I'd come here because of her, but I couldn't remember the rest of it, couldn't remember why.

Then I started walking, trying to keep in my mind the thought that I had to get out, get away from Greenhaven, forget everything else except getting away. It had seemed cold at first, but my body felt warm now and I was dizzy, lightheaded. It was almost as if I were floating, and I thought with amusement that maybe I could float over the wall. I staggered and stumbled like a drunk, getting a kick out of it; I thought it was funny. It was like walking through a crazy dream.

I found a table, placed it next to the wall, and put a chair on top of it. A siren wailed somewhere, got louder as I climbed onto the table and then the chair, rolled over the wall. I landed heavily but got to my feet and trotted, stumbling, toward my car. The siren was loud as I reached my Cad, turned the keys still in the ignition, and started the motor. When I was a block away, driving without lights, a police car screeched to a stop back at the Greenhaven gate.

I awakened suddenly, head pounding, my thoughts swimming and jumbled. Pain seared my spine and my movements were restricted, my body cramped. Slowly memory came back to me. Moments before my eyes had closed and stayed closed I'd pulled off the road into brush, and turned off the lights and motor before falling across the seat.

I was on my back, lying on the floor boards of my car. I must have rolled in my sleep, fallen from the seat to the floor boards, and suddenly awakened. I pulled myself behind the steering wheel, looked at my watch. It was only eleven P.M. I'd slept little more than an hour. My muscles were stiff, cramped, and a throbbing ache pulsed inside my skull.

The boodstained shirt stuck to me as I peeled it off, traced the cut with my fingers. The cut was deep in only one spot; the rest of it was a shallow gash halfway across my back. It wasn't dangerous, only painful, and the bleeding had stopped. From the Cad's trunk, where I keep everything from electronics equipment to spare .38 cartridges, I got a crumpled cloth jacket and slipped it on.

Miles away a siren shrilled. Undoubtedly that cop car that had pulled up at Greenhaven as I left had been called out because of me. Since then the police must have been looking for me—looking, I realized, for an escaped nut. That wouldn't make the next hour or so any easier, because I knew I had to go back to Greenhaven.

A few minutes later I stopped at an all-night diner, bought a quart container of black coffee, and drank it in the Cad as I drove. By the time I reached the rear of Greenhaven I felt halfway alive, the short sleep and hot coffee having cleared some of the fog from my brain. I parked off the road in darkness beneath some trees, left the ignition key in place, and dropped the other keys from the ring into my pocket. From the Cad's trunk I got a twenty-foot length of rope. Trees grew outside Greenhaven's rear wall, and it was easy to tie the rope to a limb and throw the line inside; nobody was worried about people sneaking into Greenhaven. I had to jump from the tree limb to the wall's top, then hang onto the rope as I slid down inside the grounds. I left the line hanging and walked toward the building.

A cold fog, heavier now, swept against my face and beaded on my skin as I walked over wet grass. There was no illumination on the grounds at this hour, and only a few lights showed through curtained windows a few yards ahead of me. At the building's rear I turned right. Cement steps led up to a closed door, and I skirted them, then went toward the first of two windows behind which light showed dimly. I thought the second window was the chief psychiatrist's office, where I'd been earlier. The shade inside was pulled, but a thin slice of light pressed past its lower edge and fell on grass ahead of me. I'd seen filing cabinets in there; Hunt's name, maybe Dixon's —and by now I was thinking perhaps even Felicity's— might be in them. One thing was sure: I couldn't ask people questions this trip.

There was a faint noise behind me, a soft, sharp click. I turned, but there was nothing nearby. Then there was a soft noise again; something grunted. Movement stirred a few yards away in the darkness.

The door at the top of stone steps I'd passed moments before swung outward with unnatural slowness. I heard the grunting sound again as I crouched on the grass, pressing against the wall. My leg muscles tightened and I could feel my heart beating heavily. There was a swirl of movement, soft scraping sounds—and then I could hear, and dimly see, the door swing closed.

A shadow glided down the stone steps, and muscles tensed at the base of my skull; there was a slight movement of hairs upon my neck. The shadow moved away and I stood erect and followed it, trying to see who it was —or *what* it was. Because it was a strange shadow that couldn't be a man. It was an upright blob topped by another mass of darkness, like a misshapen letter T. And then the shadow passed before a beam of light slanting from one of the windows and I saw that it was a man.

It was a man with his left arm stretched up, light sparkling from his hand, and I remembered a sparkling diamond on a hand that earlier had gripped a knife or scalpel. The man walked easily through the light, slightly bent forward, and I could see what had made the shadow seem so unreal. He carried something upon his shoulder, arm stretched up to clasp it tight, and the thing had looked in my one brief glimpse of it like something wrapped in cloth or in a blanket.

It had looked, I thought, like a body.

40

Chapter Seven

THE MAN DISAPPEARED beyond the glow of light. My mind
wasn't functioning normally, I knew, because of the drug
and my weariness combined, and for seconds I stood un-
decided what to do. The clang of metal on metal decided
me. I ran forward and reached an unlocked gate as a car
motor started outside. The car raced forward.

A minute later I was in my Cad, following where the
other car had gone, but I couldn't see a thing in the road
ahead. In a few seconds lights suddenly flicked on, blocks
beyond me. I drove without my own lights, not trying to
lessen the distance between us. After half a mile he turned
left.

A minute later I swung into a narrow dirt road where
he had turned shortly before. His car was empty, facing
me, when I passed it; yards beyond it I turned in the road
and parked. The fog had turned into a soft drizzle of rain
and we were near no lights, no houses; this area was barren except for brush and trees.

Damp earth slanted upward as I walked away from the
road, moving rapidly for a few yards, then pausing to listen. But I heard nothing. In my hand I carried a flashlight that I meant to use only when I found the man, and
blackness was almost complete. When I heard a sound
other than those I made myself, it was higher up the slanting ground ahead of me. I ran toward it, barely avoiding
trees that loomed before me. Then I stopped, and heard
the sound again. It was the sound of digging, and I knew
the man was digging a grave.

I started walking again and there was the sound of a
shovel's blade driven into soft earth, and then the hiss as
earth slid from the blade and fell with a soft splattering
thud. There was silence again. I stopped, stood motionless with my head turned to one side, listening, and heard
a whisper of sound. I walked on slowly. A minute passed;
a twig snapped somewhere nearby and I swung around,
waited. When I stepped forward again, my right foot sank
into softer ground, into earth that had been freshly
turned.

41

But the only sound was rustling branches over my head, the whispering of rain. When I heard a car motor start and roar I didn't know what it meant at first. Then I realized he'd been here and gone—and that I hadn't seen his face.

I ran. His headlights were cutting through the darkness, then reached the highway, turned back toward Greenhaven. I stumbled and fell, got up and ran again, puzzled, not understanding. There had been too little time for him to walk up that hill, dig a grave, and bury whatever he had carried, then fill the grave and leave again.

There was a dull ache in my chest when I reached the Cad. His lights were out of sight. I drove back to Greenhaven with the accelerator down, but I didn't catch him. His car was already parked where it must have been before, and his figure was going through the same high gate he had used earlier. When I reached it, seconds after him, it was closed. None of the keys on my ring would unlock it, and I drove around the corner, parked where I'd been before, went over the wall again where the rope dangled inside it. As I turned and started to run across the grounds, light flashed from inside one of Greenhaven's halls. Somebody went through the door and closed it quickly, smothering the light. I ran to the door, jerked it open. The corridor was empty.

It stretched the length of the building before me, silent and bare, the polished floor gleaming dully from white lights overhead. I walked down half its length; on my right was the big entrance through which I'd first come last night, the doors closed. Just beyond the corner ahead was the wire-enclosed room in which I'd seen bins containing boxes and clothing.

I walked to the room, peered through the heavy wire. Probably my coat and gun were in one of those compartments now, but I couldn't see them. A frail-looking metal door, crisscrossed with wire, was on my left. It was locked; and when my keys failed to work I wound my fingers in the wires at its top, put one foot against the screen near it, and yanked with all my strength.

The sound rattled down the hall. The ripped flesh on my back burned suddenly and blood seeped from the cut again. But the door was sprung. I yanked again and the lock scraped and grated, then the door came open. My coat was in an upper bin, the gun and my wallet inside

42

it. I checked the .38, made sure it was still loaded, then took off my cloth jacket, strapped on the gun and holster, shrugged into my coat.

No one was in the hall as I walked down it to the door marked, "Dr. Nichols, Chief Psychiatrist." There wasn't any light behind it and one of my skeleton keys worked. Inside I flipped on the lights; the room was empty. I walked to the filing cabinets.

There were hundreds of cards, alphabetically arranged. None had the name Gifford or Dixon on it, but I found one card bearing the name Hunt, Randolph. Under "Room" was the notation "114EW." I was in the east wing of Greenhaven now.

Room 114 was nearby, across the hall and halfway to the main entrance. The door wasn't locked and the room was in darkness. I felt along the wall and found the light switch, flipped it on, glanced around. Against the left wall was a bed. A guy lay in it, covers halfway down his chest. He was snoring.

I shoved the door closed behind me and the guy snorted a couple of times, smacked his chops, and raised up on one elbow. He said, still half asleep, "That you, Dixie? Hey?" He blinked and squinted in the bright light, then his eyes focused on me and he said, "Who in thunderation are you?"

He was firm-fleshed, husky, sharp-featured, and absolutely bald. I walked to the side of the bed and said, "Are you Randolph Hunt?"

"That's me." He squinted. "You a doctor, young fellow? Well, don't get no notions. Don't go givin' me no enemas or nothin'. I ain't here for treatment. You look on my card and—"

"Whoa, Mr. Hunt. I'm not a doctor."

"Then who the hell *are* you, son? You took a year off my life wakin' me up so sudden. Cain't afford no *more* years off my life, that's for—"

I interrupted. "Hold it, Hunt. Listen to me a minute."

"Don't you tell me what to do, boy." I tried to get a word in edgewise, but he cut me off. "Maybe you don't mean no harm. Just that I got tired of people tellin' me what to do. That's why I like it here; do any fool thing you feel like so long as you don't hurt nobody else."

"Where's Felicity Gifford?"

That stopped him in mid-sentence with his mouth open.

43

Slowly he closed it, then said, "Felicity? What made you ask me that, son?"

"I'm Shell Scott."

He rubbed his bald head, nodded slowly. "You was in the paper. Detective feller."

"That's right. I talked to your niece, Jo Perrine, earlier. She said you read that article about me and Felicity—and your gal friend Dixon—and took off. So now you can tell me why."

He frowned. "Don't really have no connection, son. I cain't help you no way."

For a couple of minutes he was evasive, but I was going to get his story if I had to sit on him. I said, "How about this Dixon gal? She thin, fortyish, black mole on her cheek?"

"That's Dixie, nurse here. Gladys Dixon. Come out to see her but she wasn't here, don't get on till twelve, so I got me a room. Figured on seein' her later." He squinted at me. "Hey, how'd you know where to find me?"

"Talked to a . . . girl friend of yours and she thought you might be here. Gal named Olive Fairweather."

"Oh, Lordy," he said. "Plumb forgot that little dear."

"Yeah, she was expecting you. Wants to see you."

"Oh, Lordy," he said. "Should have gone there instead."

"O.K., Hunt. Why did you come out here?" He hesitated again and I said, "Maybe I'd better wise you up." I told him what had happened since I first hit Greenhaven. "There's a reason somewhere. And I threw Felicity's name—and yours—around a little when I arrived. Maybe it doesn't mean anything, but Dixon works here; Felicity wrote the name Dixon down after a phone call Friday night. Add it up yourself." I paused and added, "I don't know what this means, either, but half an hour or so ago some guy hauled a body away from here and buried it."

For maybe half a minute he was silent. Then he said, "All right, son. Still don't know it's worth mentionin', but you listen a spell." He told me about meeting Olive Fairweather at a Trammelite meeting; she was a fervent follower. They'd then started going together. "Well," he said, "we got along pretty good, and . . ." He swallowed, then said suddenly, "Hell, I brought Olive here to Greenhaven because she was about to have herself a baby."

"You mean she had—"

44

"I mean we come here for an abortion. Here's where I met Dixie. She's the one fixed it up." He frowned again. "Olive's name's Miss Fairweather, not Mrs., and not Mrs. Hunt, neither. Not that it mightn't of been, under the circumstances, but the circumstances was what made it impossible, Olive declared. Right fine woman, Olive is—but hell, that's neither here nor there, son."

I'd been quiet while he talked, letting his words sink in. Now I said, "Damn it to hell. Anybody in on the deal with Dixon? Working with her?"

"Don't know. Olive would."

I got a little more from him. Hunt had met Felicity at Trammelite meetings, talked to her several times, and liked her a lot. When he'd read the story in today's Ledger, added to his natural concern was his knowledge of Gladys Dixon's racket, and he'd come here mainly to ask her if there was any connection, if the name in the paper referred to her.

"Don't really suppose it did," he said, "but just in case, I wanted to know. Maybe I could help with money or somethin'. Got more money than I know what to do with. Jillion oil wells."

"How'd you find out about Dixon in the first place?"

He rubbed his head. "Well, you know it ain't nothin' out of the ordinary happened to Olive and me. Happens hundreds of times every day. But we're still livin' in the dark ages, I guess. Cain't just go to a doctor and say you want an abortion. Be ten thousand people that's got nothin' better to do than trying to run everybody else's lives, and they'd put you in jail, or shoot you or somethin'." He sighed. "Well, I asked around kind of sneaky, feelin' like I'd stole the crown jewels, spent a bit of money, and finally heard about Dixie and this place. Come out and talked to her and fixed it up. Then brought Olive here. Since then I come out a few times just to jolly Dixie."

He didn't know anybody else here who might have been involved, and couldn't tell me who Dixon worked for or where I could find her. He said, "It ain't much, son, but that's the whole story. Oh, there was that name in the papers, but I come here tonight mainly just to see Dixie, I guess. We get along pretty good. Well, it do you any good to know?"

"Maybe, Mr. Hunt. I'd like to hear what Olive could tell us, and I wish I had more time to talk to you, but

I've got some things to do. Anyway, thanks, Mr. Hunt."

"Shucks, don't go formal on me, boy. Call me Randy. That's what the gals call me." He grinned again. "That's because I'm a randy character."

He looked pretty randy at that, bald head and all. Dressed up, he must have been a sight to see. I'd thought my clothes were colorful, but scattered about the room were a gruesome yellow sports shirt covered with brilliant fighting roosters leaping about, green suspenders attached to blue slacks, and a pure white sports jacket with huge saddle-stitched pockets. On the floor were tan and white oxfords and on a table by the bed was a black Homburg.

I went to the door. "O.K., Randy."

He cleared his throat. "Say, Olive was . . . expectin' me, you said?" I nodded and he squinted at me. "Remember what she was wearin', son?"

I grinned at him. "Yeah. A serape."

He rolled his eyes up toward the ceiling and clapped a hand to his head. "Oh, Lordy," he said.

I looked out into the empty corridor, then started walking toward the main entrance. I was almost there when at the west end of the building a door leading into that wing opened and a guy came out. I didn't have a chance to duck around the corner out of sight because he was in a hurry, actually trotting down the hall. There wasn't anything to do but keep walking casually ahead and hope whoever it was didn't know me.

When he got close I saw his face, the big bulbous nose and rimless eyeglasses—just as he looked squarely at me and his mouth dropped open. It was Dr. Wolfe—who thought I was an escaped maniac.

Chapter Eight

WOLFE WENT FROM A TROT to a run when he passed me, and veered toward a door standing slightly ajar as I sprinted after him. He leaped into the room and the door started to close. A moment before it clicked shut I slammed my shoulder against the door and threw it open. I stumbled inside, and yelled, "Hold it, Wolfe."

He was jumping toward a phone on his desk, but he

froze, looked over his shoulder, and spotted the gun in my hand. He stood motionless, staring at the revolver, his mouth still open and his eyes wide and frightened.

I kicked the door shut and said, "Stand still, Wolfe. You're not going to get hurt. Just don't let out a peep."

He turned and backed slowly away from me until he bumped into the desk. A small wooden triangle, a few papers, the phone, and a carafe of water were on the desktop; the wooden triangle bore the name "Dr. Frank Wolfe." He looked scared silly, his face white.

"Just ease over and sit down," I said. "Stay away from the phone and don't even think about yelling."

He sat gently in the swivel chair behind his desk. I hooked my foot under a straight-backed wooden chair, slid it in front of him, and straddled it. Keeping the gun pointed at his nose, I said, "Let's get one thing straight: I'm not even slightly goofy, I'm as sane as you are, but there's something crazy going on in this fit factory and you're going to tell me all you know about it."

He kept moving his head slightly to the left and then right again, eyes riveted on the gun. He wasn't much good to me, scared as he was, but I kept the gun on his nose anyway. "Just get used to it," I said. "Now, give a listen." I told him exactly what had happened to me when I arrived at Greenhaven, explained how I'd wound up in the strait jacket. "So that's it," I finished. "All of a sudden those bums jumped me; somebody else clobbered me from behind. Your turn."

He jumped slightly. "What?"

As I'd talked he'd calmed down, and color had come back into his face. But the better he looked, the worse I felt. I was in lousy shape, my head throbbed, there was a small fire in my stomach, and I was shaky, nauseous. I said, "Your turn; what do you know about it?"

He shook his head rapidly back and forth. "Nothing, nothing. There was an enormous commotion, Mr. Scott, yelling and all. I ran down to Dr. Nichols' office—several people were there ahead of me—and, well, there seemed to be bodies all over the floor. That's all I know."

He explained that the guards—who were now in Greenhaven's hospital—had said I'd run amuck, and that they'd had to manhandle me. I asked him, "Who was there ahead of you?" He named several doctors and nurses I'd never heard of, and I said, "How about Dr. Nichols?"

"She arrived when I did. Everything was confused . . ."

47

"You're telling me."

He laughed and appeared relaxed for the first time. "You— Couldn't you put the gun away?"

"No."

His pleasant expression faded slightly and he licked his lips. "I'm quite convinced of your sanity, Mr. Scott—now. Actually, you didn't make the best initial impression on either Dr. Nichols or me. She said that when she first saw you, you were, ah, chasing a ball."

That got a small chuckle out of me. Dr. Wolfe extended one hand slowly toward me. "Please note, Mr. Scott." His hand was trembling. "You gave me quite a shock a minute ago and I'd like a drink of water for an exceedingly dry throat. I wouldn't want you to get excited." His eyes were on the gun. Naturally; his eyes hadn't been any place else so far.

"Go ahead."

He picked up the carafe and a glass from the tray, poured water to the accompaniment of clink, clink, clink from his shaking hand, gulped the drink, and sighed. I was about to ask him to clink another for me when the door behind me opened. I jerked the gun back against my chest, swung my head around, nerves jangling all through my body. A white-uniformed woman stood in the doorway. She was tall and heavy-framed. I'd never seen her before. She didn't seem at all surprised to see me. She just looked tired and sleepy.

"I'm leaving now, Doctor," she said. "Unless you need me."

"Nothing more," he said. "Good night."

She kept staring past me, and I thought there was an expression of surprise on her face for a moment. Then she turned and started to leave. I swung my head back toward Dr. Wolfe as the door closed, thinking he might be pulling a gun out of a desk drawer, or even jumping toward me. He was just pouring himself another glass of water. Maybe I'd imagined that she'd looked surprised. But my heart was pounding again, my throat so dry it ached.

I said, "What about that nurse? If she starts screaming—"

"I don't think there's any worry there. She could hardly have seen you before. And, too, I can vouch for you now while I couldn't have earlier." His brows lowered as he added, "You look quite pale, Mr. Scott. Are you all right?"

"Yeah, I'm O.K. Just a little beat."

48

He pushed the water carafe toward me. "Would you like a drink? You look ill."

I poured a drink into another glass with my left hand; the water eased the dryness in my throat a little, cooled the small fire still in my stomach. Then I took a breath and went on: "In a minute you're going to use that phone and call the people I tell you to. I want to talk with both those stupid guards and find out who popped my skull, for one thing."

He shook his head and held forth a while about how strange this all was, until I cut him off. "Right now, though, I want to know about Nurse Dixon. Where is she, who does she work for?"

"She comes on at midnight, Mr. Scott. She works for Dr. Yancey. You met him."

"Uh-huh. There are a few other things I want to hear you talk about, too. While I was in that strait jacket somebody tried to stick a knife in me. And not long ago a body was lugged away from here and buried. Besides that, what do you know about Dixon's doing abortions here in Greenhaven?"

He seemed shocked, unbelieving, and started protesting, but his words sounded funny to me. It wasn't so much what he said, but the fact that the words themselves seemed soft, muffled. I shook my head to clear it, wake up a little more, but still I could hardly hear him. "Knock it off," I said. "Get the mush out of your mouth." The words sounded stupid; I couldn't remember what I'd asked him. He stopped speaking.

I said, "Listen. I told you somebody tried to kill me. Somebody here. Start with that."

He was looking at my face. His mouth moved but I heard only parts of his speech. ". . . narrow it down . . . records . . . never any difficulty . . . no violent patients . . . freedom here . . ."

He paused, looking steadily at me, then began speaking again. I couldn't understand what he was saying. The idea seemed silly, but I felt as if I'd been drugged again. Couldn't have drugged me, I thought. I was looking at him all the time. Then I remembered taking my eyes off him when that nurse had come in, tried to think back to that moment. It was an effort to hold my head erect. Wolfe's voice seemed to swell and fade. Light bounced from the lenses of his glasses.

Neither of us had spoken for what seemed a long time.

I said, my tongue thick, "Shut up. Felicity. Felicity Gifford. That's why I came here. Tell me . . ." I couldn't hang onto my thoughts, couldn't put them in order.

"You do look ill," he said. "Have some water, Mr. Scott." He pushed the carafe toward me. "Perhaps you should lie down."

His face was sober; he stared fixedly at me. I looked at the carafe, at the water glass in front of him. It was full; he hadn't drunk any of his second glass, the one he'd poured after that nurse had come in. I reached for the carafe, poured my glass full again, my fingers numb. Tiny white grains swirled in the bottom of the glass, grains from whatever I had drunk before. The water seemed milky.

I straightened in the chair. Weakness licked at my muscles as I looked over the room—and saw something I hadn't noticed before. In the corner stood a wooden clothes tree. Dangling limply from it was a dark raincoat; drops of water glistened on its surface. On the floor beneath it sat a pair of rubbers, their soles muddy. I looked at my own shoes, at the dirt and mud on them from that lonely hill where something, someone, had been buried. Then I looked at Dr. Wolfe. He stared silently back at me.

"You sonofabitch," I said. I thumbed back the hammer of my .38 and he pulled his lips tight against his teeth and babbled something. "Put your hands flat on the desk," I told him.

He flopped them on the desk; they lay there shaking as if they weren't a part of him. There was a ring on the little finger of his left hand, its big diamond glittering, sparkling as his hands fluttered.

Finally I understood his words. "Don't, don't, don't," he was saying over and over.

"Shut your face. Who was it—"

The door clicked open behind me, banged against the wall. Wolfe jerked his eyes from my face. I swung my head around, the movement slow and un-co-ordinated. It was a woman again, walking toward the desk, a different woman, but also in a white uniform. She said, "Frank, did you—"

Her voice faltered, stopped as she saw me. She was short, thin, thin-faced, and a big black mole grew on her cheek. It was Nurse Dixon. She was so close to me that I could see stiff hairs jutting from the mole, see the fixed, rigid expression into which her sharp features had congealed.

Suddenly she whirled on her heel and left, pulling the

door shut behind her. I yelled at her, tried to stand up—
and fell. My legs wouldn't support me and my sight was
blurring.

I was sprawled on my back, still clutching the gun but
with my arm against the floor at my side, my finger curled
around the .38's trigger. Wolfe was beyond the desk and I
couldn't see him. I didn't even know if I could stand, and
as I started to try getting up I changed my mind, and lay
quietly with my eyes almost closed. In a moment, looking
from under my lids, I saw Wolfe stand, his face seeming
to swell like a balloon and get small again. He looked at
me, then went across the room to a cabinet against the
wall, opened it, took something out, and fumbled with it.
Then he walked toward me.

His figure shifted and blurred, and then he was over
me, bending down, and I saw a hypodermic syringe in
his hand, saw a drop of fluid that formed and dropped
from the needle's slanted hollow tip.

I tried to bring the gun up toward him but wasn't even
sure my arm was moving. But I saw his expression change,
heard him shout. I forced myself to squeeze the muscles of
my right hand together, felt my index finger tug at the
revolver's trigger, and heard the boom of the gun.

His body jerked. His mouth was wide and I heard the
high sound he made. The syringe dropped from his hand
and I tried to get off my back, the gun held before me,
pointing toward him. I rolled onto my left elbow, darkness gathering, but I could see him as he fell, his head
noiselessly striking the carpeted floor. With the last of my
strength I crawled closer to him, forced my right arm forward until the muzzle of my gun rested against his skull.

Then I couldn't see him. I was looking into a thicken-
ing darkness; but I heard a soft report as I squeezed the
trigger, felt the slow, gentle recoil of the gun in my hand.
Then darkness grew, turned to blackness.

Chapter Nine

SUDDENLY THE LIGHT was blinding. It slammed into my
eyes painfully, and I squeezed them shut, opened them
slowly, then started to shade them with my right hand.

51

My left hand moved, tugged by the other one. I stared at metal handcuffs on my wrists, then looked around the room.

I was still in Wolfe's office, seated in a leather-covered chair—but now I saw two uniformed policemen, who must have come out from nearby Raleigh. One of them, a fat, flabby-faced sergeant with a big red-veined nose, squatted on the floor near me; I could smell whisky on his breath. The other, a patrolman, leaned against the wall near the door, a short cigar clamped between his teeth.

"He'll be all right for a while, Sergeant Meadows."

It was a woman speaking on my left, and I glanced around to see, still in her white uniform, the lovely Lyn. She turned from the sergeant squatting before me and stared at my face. I looked over my shoulder, but Dr. Wolfe's body had already been taken out. Stains on the carpet, though, showed where he had been.

"Yeah," the sergeant said, his voice twanging nasally, "he's gone. Only he didn't walk out." He glanced questioningly up at Lyn and asked, "This goofball know what I'm talking about?"

"I imagine he does." A note of annoyance was in her voice.

"Wait a minute," I said to her. "Of course I know . . . Oh, Lord." I had just realized she'd hardly be thinking of me as a highly stable personality. Her first glimpse of me had been when I was playing catch with that eight ball, then with the fake Dr. Nichols, and next in a strait jacket. And a little while ago she must have spotted the escaped nut lying alongside Wolfe's body. I said, "You may find this a bit difficult to grasp at first, but I'm not crazy."

The sergeant spoke to me as if I were a small, retarded child. The whisky on his breath sickened me. He sickened me.

"You want to tell us what happened?" he asked.

"I'd like to. There's quite a bit to explain."

He smirked and glanced over his shoulder at the patrolman, who shrugged and shifted the cigar to the other side of his wide mouth. Sergeant Meadows turned to me and asked softly, "You know who you are?"

"Oh, for God's sake. Of course I know who I am. I'm Shell Scott—and I'm quite sane, Sergeant. So you can forget the baby talk."

52

"Sure," he said soothingly. "Sure. Suppose you tell me the whole thing, Scott."

I started with my arrival at Greenhaven, but after the second sentence I knew he was only half listening. So I spoke directly to Lyn, hoping I could at least convince her. She kept on looking sweet, lovely, attentive, and unconvinced. A few times she did frown, and press white teeth into her lower lip, but that was all.

After a couple of minutes the patrolman leaning against the wall said around his cigar, "This one's really gone, ain't he? If this ain't the craziest story I ever heard, then I'm balmy muhself." He laughed, and Meadows laughed. Lyn didn't. I didn't.

The two slobs traded a few sentences that they must have thought funny, judging by their hilarity; then Meadows looked at me, still highly amused.

"That's exactly how it happened, huh? Self-defense? You were fighting off an attack from a needle?" He chuckled.

I said as levelly as I could, "That's exactly it. As well as I can remember. Some of it's a little hazy because I . . ." The two cops were exchanging knowing glances. I said to Lyn, "Miss, they aren't listening, but you are. Don't I sound lucid, normal?" I stopped. "Incidentally, how come I'm O.K. now?" I glanced at my watch; it wasn't even one o'clock and it was still night outside.

She frowned slightly and said, "I gave you an intravenal injection, Mr. Scott. A stimulant. We couldn't awaken you, and the officers wanted to talk to you. The sergeant insisted. When it wears off you'll feel worse than if I hadn't given it to you."

"You mean I can feel worse? Before I get out of here I'll be some kind of addict."

Meadows took Lyn outside and after a bit I heard him say, "Skeezo what? Frantic?" They talked another minute, Meadows asking stupid questions, then came back.

I said to Lyn, "Listen, there's proof that Wolfe was going to squirt something into me. His hypodermic syringe was on the floor where he fell. You must have seen that when you found me."

She shook her head. "There wasn't any syringe on the floor."

"There must have been." She didn't say anything. I looked around and saw the water carafe on Wolfe's desk.

53

"That water bottle," I said. "I told you he drugged me. Check it. You'll find some kind of drug in the water. That will prove it."

Lyn asked softly, "What would that prove, Mr. Scott?"

And then I realized it wouldn't prove anything at all, just that Wolfe had sensibly attempted to subdue a maniac who was running around loose. Lyn stood near the chair, looking at me. She wasn't much taller standing up than I was sitting down, maybe five-two, and those dark eyes were a warm velvety brown; the long thick hair wasn't a fiery red, but more a soft darkness with a hint of redness in it.

Meadows and the patrolman had understandably spent almost as much time looking at her as at me, but now Meadows got up off his haunches and said, "Let's go, Scott."

That "Let's go" startled me. I knew what it meant if they took me to jail, to a cell in Raleigh. Even now, right here where it had happened, nobody believed I hadn't murdered Wolfe, either in babbling insanity or after cold premeditation. The bald statement that I'd killed him in self-defense would sound ludicrous to anyone else. It almost sounded that way to me, now.

I looked at Lyn again. "I tell you, Wolfe dropped that syringe in here. Just a few seconds before . . . I shot him, he got it out of some kind of cabinet." I looked along the wall, saw it. "That one, I guess. He took the syringe out, then filled it with something, I think."

She glanced at the officers, then at me. She went to the cabinet, took some keys from her pocket, and selected one. She opened the cabinet and picked up a small black case, opened it.

Three syringes were inside it, and there were no empty spaces. "I'm sorry," she said softly. "Don't you think you might have imagined it?"

I licked my lips and they were dry. Pain started throbbing in my head. "No," I said. "No, I didn't imagine it. Damn it, I know it happened. Are you all lying? What the hell is this?" I swallowed. "Somebody must have come in before you did, picked the thing up and put it into the case, put the case back. Dixon. Does she work for Wolfe?"

"Yes."

"Talk to her. She must have done it. She was in with him."

54

I stopped and it was quiet. The two cops looked amused. Sergeant Meadows scratched his thigh. "Guess this does it, Al;" he said to the patrolman.

I said, "It's true. It had to happen that way."

Meadows said, "Come on, let's get out of here." Al walked toward me. A pulse started beating heavily in my temples.

"I know it's hard to swallow all at once," I said rapidly, "but that's the way it happened. Look, I talked with Mr. Hunt just before I ran into Wolfe in the hall. He can tell you what we talked about, and that I was normal."

She asked me what room he'd been in and I told her. She went out, and came back in a minute. "There isn't anybody there," she said. "The bed is rumpled, but that's all."

"This Hunt," Meadows said slowly, for the first time seeming to show some interest. "Who is he? What's he look like? How'll we recognize him if we see him?"

"Randolph Hunt. Find him and talk to him. For all I know, he's still here somewhere. And you couldn't miss him. He'll be wearing a yellow shirt with roosters on it, and a white coat, and a black Homburg. And . . . Oh, nuts. The hell with it."

It was not only that Meadows and Al were about to fall down and roll around on the floor holding their sides, but that I was starting to wonder if this could really have happened. Could I have had a Technicolor dream? I realized now that Meadows had just been fishing for a laugh, and he'd got it. He was having a real belly laugh now, his breath spraying me.

I said slowly, "Shut your stupid, stinking face, mister. I'm getting goddamned tired of your eighth-grade humor."

His left hand came out of nowhere and slammed against my cheek; pain ricocheted inside my skull. I heard Lyn cry, "Stop it!" and then I was coming out of the chair with my manacled hands in front of me.

I was going to change that boy's appearance for him, but I saw the other one, near me, saw his big right fist wrapped around the gun in a holster at his hip. I was so mad that I almost went after Meadows anyway, but just in time I stopped. Meadows planted a big paw on my chest and shoved. My knees hit the chair behind me and I went down into it, and I didn't even try to get up. I was using all my energy to keep my pants on the seat. Meadows' face had hardened; he was no longer in a happy mood. But neither was I.

"Congratulations, Sergeant," I said. "Slapping a crazy man. I'll bet they promote cops in Raleigh for that. Hit me again, boy. Maybe in a couple of years they'll promote you to cretin."

I was smiling, with the best smile I had left in me, which was mostly fangs, and possibly Meadows thought he was being complimented by a suddenly cowed prisoner. He looked at Lyn, and for a couple of seconds conflicting emotions played on his face, but apparently curiosity won. "What'd he say?" he asked her.

I was surprised to see a small but obvious smile pulling at the corners of her lips. She had dimples that didn't show until her lips curved, I noticed. She glanced at me and said, "Cretin, Sergeant Meadows."

Laughter bubbled up in me, popped through my compressed lips. At the same time Lyn, noticing my near strangulation, clapped one hand over her mouth—and Meadows suddenly realized that we were both laughing at him. His face got ugly, or rather uglier.

He could hardly slap her around, but he got back at her in his own way. He grinned at her slowly and deliberately looked her over from head to feet as her face flushed. Even in the stiff white uniform Lyn's figure was almost startling; it was easy to imagine how desirable she would look in a dress that pressed close to the lush curves of her body. Or in less. And that was obviously what Meadows was imagining.

He made it obvious. Meadows got off several crude cracks, the patrolman, Al, chiming in finally. Lyn's face flamed and she swallowed. There wasn't much I could do about it, but I started to tell them to knock it off, anyway. Then I stopped, thought a moment, and said instead, to nobody in particular, "I don't feel so good."

Both men swung their heads toward me. I pressed my eyes together, shook my head, and said, "Feel lousy." I looked at Meadows, trying to appear ill, and discovered that by continuing to look at him it was easy. "I mean it," I said slowly. "Feel like I'm going to pass out." I turned to Lyn. "You gave me a shot of something, didn't you?"

"Why, yes."

I winked at her and said, "I could use another shot; think it's wearing off."

56

Her brows pulled down. I looked at the sergeant. "I feel sick as hell, Meadows. Feel like I'm gonna throw up. If I do, I mean to aim at you."

For a moment I thought he was going to clobber me again, but he didn't.

I groaned. "Oh, boy, am I sick!"

Meadows' mouth twitched. Al said, "Ah, maybe we better put this nut in storage."

I groaned: "O-o-o-hhh-h! Urp! Oh-h-h."

"Well, hell," Meadows said. He grabbed my arm and yanked. I got to my feet, slumped against him, and groaned, looking squarely at him, my face contorted. He shrank away and said to Al, "Grab this bastard's other arm."

In a couple of seconds we started out, one of them on each side of me, hanging onto my biceps. As we went out the door I twisted my head around and, while groaning softly, tossed a fast wink at Lyn. Oddly enough, she started to smile, and then we were weaving down the hall.

Chapter Ten

THE AIR WAS cool outside and a fine drizzle of rain still fell. We went through the main entrance and walked in near darkness down the graveled drive toward the gate. Meadows aid, "Listen, you bastard, get your feet under you or we'll bust you one and drag you out of here."

I'd been slumping as much as I could without falling down, but I stood straighter, weaving unsteadily, made some disgusting noises in my throat. Meadows swore.

Al said, "You want me to go out to the car and get Lester?"

"No. We both hang onto the nut."

I didn't have any real plan; I knew only that I meant to make a break before we got into Raleigh. I had to. Once a cell door clanged behind me, I might as well say good-by to the world for a while. But that remark of Al's about going to the car to "get Lester" jarred me. Two cops, even half-drunk ones, were bad enough, but three would reduce my chances nearly to zero. If I were going to make a break, it would have to be right now, immediately.

My pulse quickened, heartbeat getting heavier. Meadows was on my left, gripping my biceps tightly; Al held my other arm and his body was a bare two or three inches from mine. I waited until he started to bring his left leg forward, then I fell against him, sticking my right foot between his legs. He pitched toward the ground, swearing filthily.

Meadows' tight grip on my arm pulled him after me when I banged into Al, and as Al started toppling I got my feet planted solidly on the ground and spun my body farther to the right, grabbing my left palm in my other hand for leverage because I wanted all the strength I could get into this one.

It was beautiful. When I swung away from Meadows his hands still clung to my biceps, drawing his arm after me, and when I spun back toward him with my elbow jutting toward his belly, there was nothing in the way to stop the blow or slow it down. The hard bony point of my elbow sliced into his gut with damn near all my weight behind it, sank deep, buried itself in his fat.

As stinking breath shot from his mouth and he bent forward I raised my manacled hands high and slammed them down on his skull. The cuffs cracked against the back of his head as my knee slammed into his face, and Meadows was out, cold and completely, even while he hung momentarily in the air.

I started to spin around before Meadows hit the ground, but Al was already yelling. For a moment I couldn't see him in the darkness, could only hear his shouts, but then I spotted him outlined by light from the gate, getting up off the ground. If he'd jumped for me then, he'd probably have had me. But Al grabbed for his gun.

When his hand slapped metal I was already in the air and about a foot from him. At least, my feet were that close to him; my head was a couple of yards farther back, because I was splayed out in the air sailing at him. Al was halfway up when I got him. I tried to kick his face but missed when he twisted his body and ducked, still yelling. My shoes landed against his shoulder, but his gun went off with what seemed a hell of a noise a moment before he fell sprawling again.

I'd gambled on getting him good, finishing him fast, and when I fell sliding, slamming into gravel beneath me, I wasn't even worrying about the horrible bruises and lacerations I'd have on my fanny because I knew the next blast from Al's gun should win the argument for him. But as I got to my feet he was starting to scuttle on hands and knees away from me. Maybe he'd dropped the gun, maybe he was just clear out of his head, but one thing was sure: He was trying his damnedest to get away from the crazy man. And that made it easy.

Two fast steps took me to him; my left foot jarred against his exposed behind, twisting him over, and my right shoe made a dull, nasty sound when it landed. I didn't know exactly where it landed, but it was somewhere around his head, and it was on something solid, and it was enough.

"Meadows! Al! *Hey, Meadows!*" It was the other guy, the third cop out at the prowl car. I knelt by Meadows and fumbled through his pockets, clumsily with both hands, trying to find the keys to the damned cuffs. The cop outside yelled again and I heard his feet hit the sidewalk.

His name popped into my mind and I shouted to him, "Lester! We had to poop the bastard. Call it in." I didn't think it would stop him. It didn't, but it slowed him down. I could see him standing at the open gate, then he flicked on a flashlight and started toward me. My hands hit a key ring.

I jerked it out, stuffed it into my pocket, then turned and ran like hell. A beam of light swept over me and past; then it steadied on me and a gun cracked. I heard the slug snap by my head, and my feet started spinning around so frenziedly it seemed there was a chance I'd catch up with the bullet—and I didn't even know where the hell I was going.

I was just going away, away from that guy who was shooting at me. I hadn't thought about my Cad or the rope I'd left dangling over the wall, but now I remembered the rope, at the back wall of Greenhaven, and that's where I was headed. Hell, I was going so fast I was already there. I didn't see any rope, but I kept running parallel to the wall, and in a moment I spotted it. I held my manacled hands ready in front of me and grabbed it, going so fast that I swung off the ground and up into the air, scraping my left side against cement, figuring at this speed I'd go clear up to heaven.

But I went only halfway up as high as I needed to get and then I scraped back down, still inside, swearing, very foul-mouthed and unstrung. A gun cracked again and a bullet splatted against cement near me. I jumped straight into the air and grabbed the line near the wall's top, then yanked and swung my legs, and went up on pure adrenalin. One foot hooked the wall's top and I rolled over it as the gun cracked again, but the slug missed and I flopped to the ground outside.

I flopped hard, and I hurt, but I made it to the Cad and found the keys in the ignition, where I'd left them, and in ten seconds I was going forty miles an hour down the street. Right after that the speedometer hit ninety, and stayed there.

The windshield wipers clicked monotonously as I drove through misting rain, the handcuffs off my wrists now. This was the same road on which I'd driven earlier tonight, following that other man—Wolfe. On the drive out to the fog-blanketed hill, I'd noticed on the right of the road, a hundred feet behind a shaggy, unkempt lawn, an old barn of a house with an adjacent garage, a "For Sale" sign at the edge of the grass. And I had to hide.

In minutes there'd be police cars on this road, and on all the roads around here. All the cars from Raleigh, and cars from Los Angeles, too. This would be a big one, hot copy, a nice gruesome subject for shocked conversations. Not just a man hunt or search for a crazy man this time, but an all-out search for a homicidal maniac.

The two-story house loomed on my right and I switched off my lights, turned into the driveway. The whole place looked different than when I'd seen it before. Then, too, the house had been draped in a drizzle of rain and shrouded by darkness, but now the place looked bigger, somehow, its outlines sharper.

I stopped before the garage and got out of the car. Away from the sound of the Cad's motor I could hear, cutting through the patter of rain, the wail of sirens, two of them, one descending the scale as the other shrieked higher and higher. The garage door was padlocked, but its wood had been weakened by age and weather. When I put my shoulder against the door and shoved, the screws holding the padlock's hasp pulled easily from the rotten wood. Termites had probably infested both house and garage for years, and the whole place seemed dead, with termites eating through it, crawling through it like maggots in a dead man. Or maybe it only seemed that way to me because of what I was going to do.

I drove the Cad inside the garage and turned off the motor, unlocked the Cad's trunk, pawed around till I found what I wanted, then closed the garage door, pressed the rusted screws back into place.

A distant siren had been getting louder, and I saw head-lights far up the road. From behind the garage I watched a police car scream past with its red spotlight glowing, then I turned and walked through mud, my feet slipping and sliding in it, carrying a flashlight and a shovel.

I could tell by my weariness and sudden need for sleep that whatever stimulant Lyn had given me was wearing off; I was tired, slow of movement. I stumbled and fell in the mud. For a moment I lay sprawled on my face, muscles quivering, then a siren whined on the road near-by and I forced myself to get up.

Finally a dirt road was in front of me. In my near exhaustion I'd walked too far, passed the hill I'd been look-ing for. But I knew where I was; I'd followed Wolfe here through the rain. Behind me the hill slanted upward and I turned, started walking again. I felt sure Wolfe had been carrying a body, and I remembered he had carried it easily, though he was not a large man. The body must have been small, light; it might well have been the body of a woman.

I turned the flashlight's beam ahead of me and walked beneath trees over moist earth, and suddenly I was there. The beam of light filled the small clearing and I could see, a few yards ahead of me, the smooth and level surface of a grave. One small plot of ground about six feet long and two feet wide had the richly dark appearance of earth freshly turned and leveled, the soil all around it more firmly packed. The earth was wet, and though the rain had stopped, there was a steady murmuring patter of drops falling from leaves above me as I placed my flash-light on the ground, its beam falling on the spot where I would dig.

Exhaustion mixed with a growing nausea, and sweat oozed from my pores, then my shovel struck something soft and yielding, something buried shallowly in the ground, I dropped the shovel and sank to my knees, pawed with my hands at the moist earth.

It was a body, as I'd felt it would be. It was a woman's body, and I had expected that, too. Before brushing the concealing dirt away I paused, then pulled the light to the grave's edge so that it shone down into the hollow

61

of earth where I knelt. I could barely move; my lids were heavy and my breath came raggedly through my open mouth. I hesitated a moment more, almost as though now that I was so close to knowing what was here I didn't want to see her face. Then I pawed at the dirt, thrust my hands beneath her shoulders, and pulled her toward me. In the harsh light slanting down upon her I saw clots of dirt slide from her features with a slow ugliness like flesh sloughing from bone.

And then I saw her face.

I shoved her violently from me, jerking my hands from her shoulders and letting her fall, my eyes wide and staring at her. She fell with a soft rustling sound, head twisting awkwardly to one side so that her dirt-filled eyes seemed to look at me. I must have knelt there without moving for a full minute, then I forced myself to think back to the moment when I'd followed Wolfe here before.

I *had* followed him. That must have happened. I closed my eyes, pressed my palms against them. I had followed Wolfe here. He had buried the body, gone back to Greenhaven. There I'd talked with Hunt, then with Wolfe. I had seen the strange nurse, and then Nurse Dixon. I had fired a bullet into Wolfe's brain, and next awakened with the police and lovely Lyn around me. After that I'd run, come here. And all the while the body Wolfe had buried had been lying here in the ground.

That was the way I remembered it; it was real and true in my mind. So I couldn't have seen the face I thought I'd just seen, not if I were sane. I'd made a mistake a minute ago, let my mind play tricks on me.

But when I opened my eyes again, everything was the same; it was still the same face.

Chapter Eleven

THERE WAS AN OPEN, level plain, its baked earth steaming in the sun and traced with jagged cracks. Dozens of tiny figures danced and whirled on the dry earth, their movements sending up swirling ribbons of dust. The figures were strange, with thin, spindly bodies and enormous heads. I could hear the grating of monotonous laughter from all their open mouths.

And I could see myself, with a grotesque, balloon-like head perched on a body of string. Mine was the only figure that was still; all the others raced around me. I could see them from where I stood on that plain, but also from another place, here outside and above it, seeing them all and myself as well.

The others ran around me, laughing, pointing at me, and all of them had faces that I knew: Lyn laughing and pointing and winking, Jo Perrine, Arthur Trammel shouting and praying and drooling, Olive Fairweather clutching her serape, Mrs. Gifford with her fat jiggling like jelly, and Felicity laughing and then crying and then laughing again.

All of them were there except Nurse Dixon. But I saw the entire picture through a huge transparent face that filled the sky, an ugly, bony face, cheekbones thrusting through tight-stretched skin, and a great black mole crawling over it like a soft round slug. It was a liquid face, shimmering and melting, forming and re-forming, always there before me.

I started to run, not to get away from the others, who followed and surrounded me, but to get away from that face. Then I felt my body roll, turn on the ground, and woke relieved to know that it had been a dream.

I awoke, sun overhead slanting down through branches of the trees above me and searing my face. I lay in the clearing, mud encrusted on me, body stiff and cramped. I moved, feeling the tug of stiff, still tired muscles, and knew that I had been dreaming, was not dreaming now, but the face was still before me. It melted and sagged and shimmered in front of my eyes. I could see stiff black hairs jutting from the ugly mole. The face seemed to balloon to preposterous size, then it shrank, and finally it was still.

In that moment of waking my mind wouldn't function, and for a long minute I stared at the face of Nurse Dixon. It was motionless now, not shimmering or transparent, but solid and real, and I could see the sharp blood-drained features, pointed chin, dirt-filled eyes. It was as though the sockets in her skull had been filled with mud that had hardened and dried.

I was on my stomach, head turned toward her. She lay propped against the side of the shallow grave, half out

63

of it. One hand was pressed beneath her body, now rigid in death, almost as if she had been trying to climb free of the ground and had been frozen in the moment of escape.

Then came the memory of those last moments of consciousness, the memory of my confused thoughts when I'd seen Dixon's face. I'd thrust her from me, then finally grasped her shoulders again to stare uncomprehending at the lifeless features, left her resting half out of the grave while I crawled a few feet away. I'd known then that I had followed Wolfe here and listened while he buried her; and *after* that I'd seen her when she'd burst into his office at Greenhaven. A minute or two later I had killed Wolfe. I knew I had killed him. I'd known it as I succumbed to weariness and the need for sleep. I knew it now.

Suddenly I was conscious only of my weakness and a gnawing hunger. The sun had started down the western sky; I'd slept for at least twelve hours. I got slowly to my feet, knees watery, and stood straight. With my back to the stiff corpse of Miss Dixon I stretched, worked the rest of the ache from my body. Then I toppled the late Miss Dixon back into her grave, covered her up, and got the hell out of there.

While walking, I thought of Dr. Wolfe and Miss Dixon —logically now, not as a dead man gadding about and a dead woman who appeared before me after burial—and I soon had several facts that led to some logical conclusions. One was that there must be a third person, somebody still alive, a man or woman who could answer questions. And that third person must have known, and would know now, where Wolfe had been around eleven-thirty or so last night when I'd followed him through the rain; would know what Wolfe had done and maybe why.

My Cad would be hotter than a strip teaser's tassel by now, so I kept walking until I reached an isolated service station. In the washroom I cleaned up the best I could, then waited for the attendant to start servicing a car and went inside. The cops had taken everything from my pockets, including money, but I found the station's private phone under a counter and got the operator and then the number I wanted at the Los Angeles City Hall.

When a woman's voice answered I said gruffly, "This is Sergeant Benton. Who've I got?"

"June. Hi, Tom. What you want?"

I knew June, and she knew me slightly. I tried to make

my voice even gruffer. "I'm out in Raleigh now, June. Got a lead on some M heists to a place called Greenhaven —you know, where Scott flipped his wig."

"Yeah. So what?"

"So get me all the phone calls out of Greenhaven from eight o'clock last night, say, to around two A.M. I'll need to know what phones they came from, too."

"Want me to call you back?"

"I won't be here. Call you in half an hour, O.K.?"

"Sure, Tom. I'll try to get it by then. Greenhaven, huh?"

"Yeah. Uh, what you think of that Scott? Funny, huh?"

"It figured. I always thought he was a little goofy." She laughed. "He sure tore it this time, though, didn't he, Tom?"

"Yeah," I said. "He sure tore it." I hung up and left.

In thirty minutes I came back and called June again. She reported that there had been only four calls from Greenhaven during the time I'd specified. Two had been from Larchmont 8-4426, which was the chief psychiatrist's number, and two had been from Larchmont 8-4429—Dr. Frank Wolfe's phone. I wrote the times down as June rattled them off, knowing that if she'd guessed I wasn't Benton, there'd be a lot of activity going on as this call was traced.

Calls had gone out from Wolfe's phone at nine-sixteen and nine-forty. They were to the same Davenport number, but there had been no later call—none around the time Wolfe had been digging that grave. I swore to myself; my bright idea hadn't told me a thing. Maybe it hadn't been so bright after all.

I said, "O.K., where'd the call from this psychiatrist's phone go?"

"Police department there in Raleigh. Both calls."

"How about the other two?" I was just going through the motions, the way Benton would have, but as I asked the last question I remembered that around nine-twenty or a little later I'd been in my strait jacket—and had damn near been killed. Both calls had been close to that time, one just before and one afterward. I didn't think it meant anything.

"That Davenport number," June said, "is listed for Arthur Trammel."

I was quiet for so long, staring at the phone, that June called me Tom twice before I snapped out of it, thanked her, and hung up. I stood there another minute, my brain vibrating like a tap dancer's fanny, then glanced at the station attendant, who was still puttering outside, and dug out the phone book. There wasn't any car out there now, and the attendant was looking at me, frowning a little. I hoped it was only because I was using his private phone, but I had to use it again, anyway. I was about to become a Trammelite, starting tonight, and I needed some help and information. A number was listed for an Alice Perrine.

I dialed it, and the voice that answered was a soft, husky whisper, so I knew it was Jo, the inventor of cleavage. After a little disconnected dialogue she told me that Hunt had got home in the middle of the night and told her about seeing me. No matter what anybody said, she didn't really think I was a maniac. The papers were full of Shell Scott; Arthur Trammel in particular had said several unkind things about me.

I broke in, "Yeah, I can imagine. Jo, baby, here's my problem—and it's concerned with Trammel. I've got to find out everything I can about him and his cult, the whole operation. But I can't wander around much in daylight, and you and your uncle are about the only people who don't think I've run amuck. Is there some way I can meet you guys? I'd like to have a big chat with Mr. Hunt."

"Where are you?"

"I'm . . . in the sticks right now. Service station." I looked at the guy outside. "And I'm leaving. This egg is eyeballing me too intently at the moment." He was.

"I'll have Uncle pick you up." She laughed throatily. "He doesn't think you're crazy either. Says you aren't even half as crazy as he is."

We settled the location, a couple of blocks from the gas station, and I took off. Twenty minutes later I was crouching a few feet off the road in a clump of scratchy bushes, looking most peculiar, I suppose, when I saw a long black foreign car with white sidewall tires, pounds of chrome, monstrous headlights, and everything but a neon propeller, coming like a locomotive down the highway.

That car could belong to nobody but Randy Hunt, and when tires started screeching a block away as the car slued around, I figured he must be driving. He was.

He didn't get the mechanical monster stopped till it was half a block past me and I started running toward it as

66

he stuck his brilliant bald head out the window and yelled, "Where you at, boy? You here? Hey!"

Then he heard me whipping through the sagebrush and beamed at me. As I ran up he said, "Hop in back, son," and I got inside just in time to hear the grating of gears and feel sudden acceleration pile me voluptuously all over Jo Perrine. Ah, that was a ride. I didn't have any idea where we were going, and I was half convinced we'd never get there alive, but even if we didn't, I'd be really living till I died. Randy was sheer hell on curves.

There was a little conversation, not much. The first thing I said to Jo was "Pardon me," and she said, "It's all right," and then I said, "Woops, pardon," and she said, "You devil," and finally she didn't say anything, just laughed softly. We were dear friends by the time I heard tires screeching that same note again and felt the car swinging around in the road.

"Made it," Randy said from the front seat, piling out of the car before a log building that looked like the Cal-Neva Lodge. "Cabin of mine."

I sat there. Jo said, "Well, get out."

"Yeah, sure."

She grinned at me and mumbled something, then crawled over me and out the door. I followed right behind her. Inside, with the smell of broiling steak in my nostrils, I said, "How come you took off so fast last night, Randy?"

The two of us were in the living room seated before a big stone fireplace. The room was huge, with unadorned pine walls and a bare floor made of some kind of dark wood liberally dotted with knotholes. The only thing on the floor except furniture was a white bearskin rug before the fireplace.

Randy was resplendent in white flannels, a sport shirt the approximate color of an artist's palette, and a jacket closer to violet than anything else I could think of. Jo had gone into the kitchen and was preparing to stave off my starvation.

He said, "After you talked to me I got to thinkin' about Olive there all alone expectin' me. And I just got up and left. Had my car in the parking lot half a block down the street there, and took off."

"See Miss Dixon?"

"Nope. You see her?" I nodded. "How is she?"

"The last time I saw her she was dead."

He leaned forward, face serious. "What'd you say?"

"She was murdered. I saw her, with the top of her head caved in, and she was very dead." It was quiet for a few seconds, then I added, "Randy, you're about the only person I can talk to who might have info I want. And I think you've got an idea of my status right now."

"Just from the papers, son. That's enough, of course. I don't believe 'em," he said.

"Thanks. I can explain most of it. I think." I told him what had happened to me after I'd left him in his room, hitting the high spots.

When I finished he said, "Then you did shoot Wolfe, like it says?"

"I shot him. Not like it probably says, but because he meant to kill me. Right now, Randy, I need any information about Trammel and his operations you can give me."

He frowned. "Well, I don't know too much. Olive's what you'd call a real Trammelite, though. She knows the whole affair down there. But I'll tell you what I've seen."

He enlarged upon his original meeting with Olive. He'd gone to one of the Trammelite meetings more out of curiosity than for any other reason, just looking for something different to do. "And that was it for sure," he went on. "Never seen nothing quite like it. Regular revival meetin's, son, and I tell you, they certainly revive a man. That Trammel's got a way with words like nobody I ever heard before. Why, people was rollin' around in the aisles and yelpin'. Almost done a little rollin' myself."

"What's the pitch, Randy? I've never heard him in action. He found a new way to get to heaven, or what?"

"Well, I don't rightly know, son. You got to experience it to understand it. And maybe it's different for different people. Way it hit me, he talks so much about sin, and how many ways there are to do it, and how terrible it is to do it any way at all, that he gets you thinkin' about it. But some of it sounds so good, even from him, that your thoughts sometimes kind of run away with you. You forget how bad he says it is, and start recollectin' how good it was."

He looked about to cackle and I grinned at him. "I know the type, Randy. He's good, huh?"

"Stands up there on his stage, and the way he gets to

going, you wouldn't be a bit surprised if fire and smoke was to shoot out of his mouth. Hear him tell it, every soul in the crowd's bound for hell." He shrugged. "Well, I was in a seat alongside Olive that first time, and she was sort of squirmin' about while he spoke away, and she and me got to talkin' together. So, when the tent affair was over, the both of us went to what they call the Truth Room."

"I've seen it. That's the low black building, huh?"

"That's right. Off a little ways back of the tent. Olive and me was in this Truth Room later, sitting together, and—well, it was even more revivin' than the first one. I got all steamed up like a pants presser, to tell you the truth. And of course the lights was out. From that night on we sort of started goin' around together."

I squinted at him. "Randy, what the hell kind of an operation has Trammel got? You say the lights were out?"

"Yep. See, he gets into his speech and the lights go out slowlike, so you can concentrate on the full impact of his truth, he says, or some fool thing like that. Tell you the truth, I didn't pay too much attention at that point to what the man was sayin'."

Something he'd said had puzzled me. I asked him, "How long is the first big meeting in the tent?"

"Starts at eight and lasts about an hour."

"What about this Truth Room thing he does after that? How long does that one take?"

"Don't rightly know. Another hour, I suppose."

That would be, roughly, from nine to ten P.M., during the time Wolfe had called Trammel's number. If Trammel had been busy imparting truths, I wondered who the hell Wolfe had talked to.

Jo, her short blonde hair helter-skelter, came in with a tray of food and a stack of newspapers, put the tray in my lap and newspapers at my feet, then sat cross-legged on the bearskin rug. I dug into the steak while Randy added odds and ends as he thought of them. When I'd polished off the food, Jo took the tray into the kitchen.

Hunt said, "Like I told you, I plumb forgot to ask Olive about anybody maybe bein' in with Dixie. But I'll run into town and pick her up if you think it'll help you."

"Wouldn't hurt. Incidentally, how long was she in Greenhaven—that first time you took her there?"

"Went in that night, left the next night."

69

That was a little unusual; plenty of abortionists have the patients walk out half an hour or an hour after they arrive. Apparently they'd been especially careful at Greenhaven—careful, too, that nobody would see the patients enter or leave. I said, "I could use anything else Olive might add to what you've told me, Randy. And I'm hoping that if Dixon was in with anybody, it wasn't Wolfe. I need somebody who can answer questions; both of them are dead."

He rubbed his scalp and got out of his chair. "You got yourself pretty well messed up, looks like. O.K., son, won't take me long. I drive pretty fast."

I had to grin. He started out, then stopped and looked at me. "Hey," he said, "what size clothes you wear? Those you got on look like somethin' to scare crows out of cornfields."

They were in sad shape, all right. I tried to figure out how to pay for new clothes, since I was broke and it wouldn't do to write checks, but he said, "Thunderation, boy, quit tryin' to give me money. That's worse than throwin' sand on the beach. I got so much money I stink —and I'm gettin' along in years, son. Cain't take it with you, and if you could, what the hell good would it do you?" He cackled happily. "If I dropped down dead the gov'mint would take it all but a nickel anyhow, and use it for buyin' butter or buildin' dams in the desert. Now, what's them sizes?"

I told him. In another few minutes he was gone, after showing me where a tiled shower was and tossing me a gold-colored robe, probably made from hammered nuggets. As I undressed there was that screeching of rubber again. I wondered if Jo had gone with him.

Chapter Twelve

After a steaming-hot shower I slipped on the robe, went back into the big room, and started looking over the newspapers. Two of them had the whole story; the other one, which I looked at first, had gone to press too soon to carry the story of Dr. Wolfe's death. It bore ordinary, everyday headlines, about an ordinary theft of some more "secret" documents by some more secret Communists, but in the left-hand corner was a two-column head: "Private Detective Runs Amuck in Private Asylum."

The story was handled straight, without much exaggeration. Not that it needed any. My name was spelled right, and I was left in a strait jacket. The second paper was about the same except that by the time it was written I'd become a homicidal maniac, since without provocation I'd killed a "Dr. Frank Wolfe, member of the staff of a local rest home." The killer was still at large.

I picked up the Ledger. The headline read: "Maniac Terrorizes City." Beneath that: "Sheldon Scott Murders Brilliant Doctor."

Yeah, it was by-lined Ira Borch. The story was continued on page six. There I found a picture of me, taken a couple of years back on the City Hall steps at night after I'd been awake on a case for thirty hours, during which time I'd been bashed about somewhat. The photographer had been below me, and the light from his flash bulb had slanted upward, giving me a fierce appearance. I looked quite a bit like a madman.

The Ledger cited incidents from some of my previous cases to prove that I had always been a bit balmy, and printed a box in which my previous "murders" were listed, quite a string of names belonging to guys I'd shot. The Ledger neglected to mention that practically all of the deceased had, at the time of their sudden demises, been shooting bullets at me.

In the body of the article was a quote from that leading citizen Arthur Trammel, who reported that Shell Scott had been obviously insane yesterday when he had attacked Trammel, the Guardians, organized religion, God, and helpless puppies. Trammel and the Guardians called upon all decent citizens to give any aid they could in the hunt for "this monster."

I was sitting quietly in the deep chair, papers resting on my lap, when two hands closed around my throat. A few hours earlier, this would have caused me to drop dead of heart failure, but at the moment I merely started grinning, because the husky voice behind me was saying, "Hi, Shell."

"Hi, Jo."

The arms slid around my neck and there were various other pressures. She said, "Awful, isn't it?"

"Don't be silly. It's wonderful. Don't—"

71

"I mean those stories."

"Oh, yeah, those things."

She chuckled. "You look nice in that gold thing."

I cleared my throat. "Really? Sweet of you to say so."

She slid around to perch on the edge of my chair. Her left arm was still hanging onto my neck, and this sort of angled her toward me, or rather, since angled was a pretty foolish word for what was happening, curved her toward me. Her lips were curved in that yes-*yes* curve, which made the view almost too much.

"Shell," she said, "what's happened to you?"

"Boy, if you knew!"

"I mean, you're not like you were in the car."

"This goddamn house isn't jumping around like that car was, either. And that car, right now, is speeding like a rocket ship to get Olive and bring her back here."

"Good. Make a foursome."

"No, I'm going to ask her questions."

"Shell, look at me."

"I am looking at you."

"Look at my face." I looked up and she fixed her big green eyes on me, leaned a little closer, which put our noses maybe an eighth of an inch apart, and said, "He'll be gone a while, won't he?"

"Oh, not long. Not nearly long— Ah, he drives like a pilot."

"What'll we do?"

"Do?"

"Yes. He'll be gone a little while."

"I suppose so. We can talk, or play cards, or . . . talk about something, or—"

"I think I'll sit on your lap." Smiling, she said again, slowly, "Shell, what'll we do?"

There could no longer be any doubt that she knew damn well what we were going to do. She went on huskily, impishly, "You want me to tell you?"

"Tell me? In—words?"

"In words. Right out loud."

"What you think we should do?"

"Yes."

"Yes."

She told me.

"Well," I said, "you bet. Yes, you bet."

There is no telling what I might have said then, but Jo leaned forward and her lips brushed mine. She touched her lips to my mouth, just a feather touch, soft, gentle, and as I leaned toward her she drew back from me. At the moment when I thought she was going to get completely away, she snaked one hand behind my head and pulled our mouths together.

After that first gentle, tantalizing pressure the sudden and almost brutal contact was like an explosion.

All of a sudden she was pressing against my chest, pushing me away, and she jerked her mouth from mine. She smiled, a funny, hot, tight smile, and said, "Shell, I'll tell you something about me."

"Fine. Swell. Tell me anything."

"I'm a tease. I'm a terrible tease."

"You're what!"

"Oh, don't go all to pieces. I'm a funny kind of tease."

"Yeah? You sure are. You are an *ex*-tease. Baby, you don't know, but this sort of thing is like shooting a guy. You don't just kill a man a little—you kill him dead. You—"

She put a finger over my mouth, and I stopped, but I figured she had sure as hell better have something more sensible than that to say.

Jo said, "I mean, I like to tease you—for a little while. Just like when I kissed you. Understand? I really like it. It's more fun."

I tried to analyze that, and before I'd finished she leaned forward, brushed my lips again. It was the same routine all over, only this time she managed to keep away from me; her hand didn't go behind my head, her lips didn't press against mine. It was always almost but never all, and the shape I was in, I was about ready to give her a bust in the snoot. But despite my momentary thoughts of busting her, I wasn't about to play any game she didn't want to play. Finally I pushed her away, leaned back in the chair.

But she had that same hot, tight smile on again. "Don't get mad," she said breathlessly, and then, still smiling, she put her hands on her dress, fumbled with three buttons at her middle, and shrugged her shoulders.

The dark blue silk slid down to her waist. Then she raised her hips, pulled the dark silk over them, threw the dress to the floor. She wore nothing under it but a wisp of light blue nylon over her hips and stomach. She said softly, "Wait for me, Shell, don't rush me," and then we were pressed together. Her hands went to that nylon at

73

her waist and stripped it down, and though my eyes were closed I felt her motion as she threw it from her.

I rested my hands gently against her shoulders, let them slide down her back.

And damned if she didn't scoot out of my clutches like an eel and tear across the floor. It was the prettiest sight you ever did see, but it wasn't exactly what I had been led to expect.

"You come back here," I said. She kept on tearing about.

Well, it didn't look like I was going to do much good sitting here all by myself, so I took out after her. Apparently she did everything the way she kissed. And it was only the memory of how sensational those kisses had been, once you got one, that kept me going. She would let me catch her, but just when I'd have everything practically fixed up she would somehow wiggle away.

It wouldn't have been so bad if it had been a little room, but this was an enormous room, practically an auditorium, and all this running over a hard wooden floor was beginning to tell on me. But Jo seemed good for several more miles. The way this thing was shaping up, I was beginning to think maybe that was all she was good for.

I caught her on the bear rug and a big dreamy smile was growing on my chops—and wiggle, swoosh, and she was gone. That was the third time, and I knew exactly how a mountain climber would feel if he got practically to the peak of Everest and Everest ran away.

It had finally affected my sense of proportion. I was no longer chasing Jo. To tell you the truth, I didn't even *see* Jo. My world had narrowed down; my world excluded everything except my particular Everest. Once more I caught it, and I said to it soberly, "Look. Listen. Goddamnit. Look."

I said, "You fly through the air again and—well, you just keep on going, see? I won't follow you. Hell, there'll be no point in my following you. We haven't got all day, you know."

I shut up for a moment, mainly because I had no breath left at all. Everest stayed right there. This was it.

A little later my thoughts got disjointed, and I was even carrying on a kind of mountaineering dialogue with myself: Man, what a stupid thing this mountain climbing is, after all; takes you nine years to get up there, and before you know it you're right back at the bottom. So you've been there; so what? What you want to climb it for in the first place? Ah, you fool—because it was there!

All of a sudden there was a noise like that of a space ship landing and Jo said the first intelligible words she'd spoken in quite a while. "Oh, Lord. Randy's back."

Up till this minute I had liked practically everything about Randy, but now I knew I had no use for the way he drove. And there I was running like a fool again—only this time Jo was behind me.

Chapter Thirteen

I HAD SCOOPED UP my robe on the way out, and when I sauntered back into the front room Randy was just coming in the front door with Olive Fairweather.

He marched up beside me carrying several packages, dropped them on the floor, and said, "That'll take care of you."

"I've been—that is, thanks, Randy. How did you manage all this in so little time?"

"Been gone over an hour, son." He peered at me. "Taken a shower, hey? Look like it rested you."

"Feel better. Better than I have in days. Weeks."

I dressed in the shower room, and since I'd told Randy to get unobtrusive stuff, I wound up looking somewhat like a pallbearer. Black suit, gray shirt, black tie, black shoes, and even a black hat and a dark raincoat. It was a perfect disguise. Nobody would recognize me in this outfit. Randy had stuck a twenty-dollar bill in a pants pocket. When I tried to thank him later he told me that was the way pants came nowadays and to shut up.

I went back into the front room and Randy, Olive, and I spent twenty minutes talking. Olive was a bit nervous at first, patting her mouse-brown hair and blinking those peculiar gray eyes at me, but she soon calmed down. The big item of information, as far as I was concerned, was that Dr. Wolfe had been Nurse Dixon's sidekick in the abortion racket. Since I felt sure that only the two of them, except perhaps for a few cab drivers and bellhops, had been in on the deal, that meant the racket was all washed up now.

By the time Olive finished telling me about Trammel-ism, I was well versed in Arthur Trammel's routine. Every night except Tuesday, Trammel's day of rest, he held a big meeting in his tent; after that there was another, smaller meeting in the black-painted Truth Room for any who wished "further instruction." Inside the Truth Room building itself was a small room at the end of a hall; this was the so-called Healing Room, and in it was held the last part of Trammel's nightly operation. There, after the final "instruction," could go anonymously any and all Trammelites in distress, or with problems and worries, for the sage advice and counsel of Trammel, the All-High. Olive also corroborated what Hunt had told me, that Trammel was always busy in the Truth Room from about nine to ten—and even after that he usually spent a half hour or so giving sage advice.

I said to her, "He doesn't know who goes to this Healing Room, then?"

"The Master?"

"The Master."

"Of course not. The Healing Room is in darkness, always."

"Do you know if Felicity Gifford ever attended those after-the-tent meetings? The Truth Room jobs?"

"Not so far as I know."

Hunt said he'd never noticed Felicity in the Truth Room at any time.

In a few more minutes they'd told me everything I thought I'd need to know. Jo had come in by then and was seated in a chair, humming. Randy stood up. "Well, I'll take Olive home."

Jo stopped humming and I saw a grin starting to grow. I looked at Randy. "So . . . so soon?"

"I'll be back in time to drive you down to the meetin'."

He left with Olive, tires screeching.

Jo said, "We're alone again."

I said, "So what?"

She laughed. And told me.

"Look," I said. "I just got all dressed, for one thing. For another, I had a tough night last night and I've got a big night coming up; and if I had any strength left, which I don't, I'd save it."

She was gurgling and moving around over there, and my voice was getting weaker. "Tell you what," I said. "You just do a dozen laps or so all by yourself while I sit

76

here and watch. It'll be something new, something different for you. Who knows? You might get a hell of a charge out of it."

Damn that woman. She knew that the way to a man's heart was not through his stomach, but through his eyeballs, and she was walking toward me, slowly, artistically, hips swaying, everything swaying.

"You're trying to sway me," I said, "but I warn you, I intend to be firm, I refuse to budge. Anyway, I'm all tuckered out, I'm pooped. Well, what do you know?"

Jo wasn't walking toward me any longer. That would have been impossible, because she was sitting on my lap. Facing me, she said, smiling, "I'm not going anywhere, Shell. So stop worrying."

"Who's worrying?"

The Trammelite grounds had a different look about them at night. It was a quarter of eight when Hunt, driving me in his car, swung into the oil-surfaced road leading to Trammel's tent, the second time I'd been here in less than thirty-six hours. Other cars were ahead of and behind us; dozens of men and women walked alongside the road and over the grass, headed for the big tent where I'd beefed with Trammel and his Guardians yesterday. It was fifty yards ahead, brightly lighted, jazzy organ music pulsing from it.

"Good enough, Randy," I said. "I'll climb out here."

He pulled over to the edge of the road and stopped. "Sure you don't want me to go in with you?"

"No, thanks. I'll let you know what happens."

I got out and he made a U turn and left. In addition to my black suit and hat, I wore the dark raincoat, collar turned up to shield my face. It wasn't raining, but already I'd seen guys dressed in everything from overalls to green suits and overcoats. I didn't expect a raincoat to set me apart.

Inside the tent I found an empty chair about halfway down toward the stage and scooted in. It was five minutes till eight, when the meeting would start, and almost all available seats were filled. I guessed that close to two thousand people were here, latecomers still straggling inside. The crowd looked like two thousand, but smelled and sounded like more.

All along the tent's left side, the bottom six feet of canvas had been raised off the ground and folded back, then

77

attached to the canvas above, so that there was a six-foot-high open space extending the length of the tent. There was nothing but blackness out there on my left now, but I knew from my talk with Randy and Olive that at eight o'clock there'd be enough light so the assemblage could feast its eyes on Trammel's customary exit from the Truth Room and his stately progress here. I'd assumed the canvas was raised so we could see him start his act, but it seemed likely now that the open space was at least partially for ventilation. The air was warm, heat from the massed bodies a cloak around me, the sound of hundreds of voices a constant murmur.

Organ music still swelled above the buzz of conversation. Draped gray cloth hung from the tent top down to the rear of the stage where I'd jawed with the Guardians. Suddenly the organ swung into a spooky number that the assembled Trammelites seemed to recognize. The buzz of conversation stopped and I heard voices singing in harmony. At the right of the stage about twenty people clothed in gray robes were singing something about the All-High. This was the choral group, in which Felicity Gifford had sung just three nights ago.

Most of the people present were looking past the open left side of the tent, and as I followed their gaze light grew until it bathed the grounds, fell on the black mass of the Truth Room, and barely touched Arthur Trammel's house beyond it.

I could see Trammel clearly as the doors of the Truth Room opened. He stepped through them and began to walk with slow, measured steps toward us. His approach was perfectly timed so that the choral group's song ended abruptly as he walked inside the tent. In silence he mounted wooden steps at the left edge of the platform.

As he reached the top step he paused briefly to pick up something on a small table, then walked to the stage's center, adjusting the thing on the front of his chest. When I saw the length of fine wire trailing out behind him, I knew that he'd picked up a portable microphone; no good revivalist these days would be caught dead without a portable mike.

Trammel stopped in the middle of the stage, faced the crowd, raised both hands palm out above his head. He stood in complete silence for a moment, then lowered his arms to his sides.

"My friends," he said.

78

It sounded familiar, but by the time I remembered where I'd heard the phrase before, Trammel was going on: "My followers, my fellow Trammelites. I bid you welcome. Welcome to the house of the All-High."

He went droning on, spouting similar stuff, all of it innocuous enough. He wore a black robe, but his face was still the same hungry-buzzard mess, even from where I sat. This far from him, those close-set eyes looked almost like one misshapen orb in the center of his narrow head; his bushy eyebrows waggled.

There was a rustle of movement at my left and I saw the plate—actually a wicker job about the size of a bushel basket—being handed down the row toward me. I was broke, and I wouldn't have dropped anything into Trammel's kitty anyway, so I passed it along, keeping my head down and hoping nobody would notice and hiss at me. I saw a lot of bills covering the change, if there was any change. While the All-High intoned the information that any offerings would be used toward completion of the Eternal House, which would "last through the ages," I estimated the average tip, multiplied it by two thousand, then by six nights, then by fifty-two weeks, and got anywhere from a couple of hundred thousand dollars to a half million. At that point I started listening more intently to what Trammel was saying. This guy was big business.

He was just starting to give the business to his followers. The plea for offerings was over, the main event was on, and it was getting sexy. I soon admitted that Hunt had been right: This stuff really revived a man. The air was heavy, thick, and Trammel's voice cut throught the silence. "Lust is the sin, the ugly sin of man. He lusts after all things, after the flesh of animals for his gluttonous belly, and the flesh of women for his evil loins. Woman, if with his hands he does not despoil your flesh, if with his body he does not violate your body, then with his eyes he strips you naked and sins on you in his mind." You would have thought he was talking about me.

Trammel's voice, usually so melodious and smooth, had become harsh, gasping. His phrases rose and fell in the time-tested chant of the revival preacher who knows how to stir the blood but not the brain. From individuals in the crowd came cries of assent and approval; cries of "Oh, Lord!" and "Amen!" and "Hallelujah!"

It wasn't difficult to guess that the women here were

experiencing, in varying degrees, a vicarious ecstasy. For I had to admit that Trammel was good; he was sensational. If this had been in one of the books Trammel was so anxious to ban, he'd have banned it in a hurry.

On my left a fat woman stared toward the stage, her dry-lipped mouth half open, her breathing gusty. Beyond her another woman wrung her hands nervously together.

Trammel was charging about now, waving his arms and screaming, his words amplified by the microphone against his chest. "We have been chosen to cleanse the land. We must seek out sin and destroy it. Only then will the Kingdom of Heaven be ours!"

There was more, much more, the age-old emotional mumbo-jumbo. Then he left the stage and walked up the left aisle, still shouting and ranting, peering into the faces of those he passed. He walked right up toward the row where I sat, and before I ducked my head down practically between my legs, I noticed that the long thin electrical cord ran out neatly behind him so that none of his words would fail to be amplified through his portable mike. He walked clear around in back and down the other aisle almost to the front row of seats before he retraced his steps, gathering up the hellishly long cord, which reached to speakers up front. Finally, though, he was back on the stage and I started breathing normally again.

By the time he finished—having included a few gasps about scarlet women and fallen women for the titillation of males present—there was more noise coming from the crowd than from Trammel.

The verbal orgy was followed by half a dozen songs, among them "Open the Gates and Let Me In," and the All-High thing, which I now supposed was Trammel's theme song. After that he called on those who were afflicted to come to the stage. At first I didn't know what he meant, but then I saw them: a man on crutches, a woman in a wheel chair, a blind man tapping the aisle before him with his red-tipped cane, a young boy with pimples on his face. Twelve people lined up on the stage.

Trammel walked among them. Trammel cried that the healing power was in his right hand, and that he, the All-High, would heal the afflicted. Then he passed his right hand over the boy's pimpled face. The pimples didn't drop off. Trammel cried that sometimes the healing power had to work for a day or two. Trammel ran his hand over the legs of the man on crutches, who threw away his crutches, took two steps, and fell down. But he was helped to his feet, tottered off the stage unaided, and took a few more steps before he sank into an aisle seat. Trammel did pull off one good job, which wasn't bad for twelve tries. He spent quite a bit of time on the blind man, shouting in a booming, hypnotic chant that he would bring sight to the dead eyes. He pressed his hands for almost two minutes over the sightless eyes, repeating over and over that when he removed his hands the man would see again.

Then he took his hands away. The man raised his eyes to Trammel's face, then slowly turned toward the crowd. For what seemed a long time he stared out toward us, then suddenly he cried aloud, "I can see! Oh, God, *I can see!*"

He turned, fell to the floor at Trammel's feet, and hugged the All-High's legs, sobbing and crying. The crowd went nuts. There were more amens and hallelujahs than Trammel had got throughout his entire speech. After that remarkable demonstration, all but one of the last four afflicted seemed to show definite improvement.

Finally the All-High theme came on again and Trammel closed with a few words about the next message soon to be heard in the Truth Room; any who cared for more of the basic truths might attend. This would be followed by confession in the Healing Room.

Then, to the strains of organ music, Trammel left the stage. The lights outside, which had been out for this past hour, now came on again, and Trammel was in plain sight as he walked away, even while skirting the roped-off area before the still incompleted Eternal House. Nobody left his seat until Trammel was inside the Truth Room. Then the exodus began.

Men and women went out arm in arm, faces flushed; teen-age kids elbowed through the crowd in a hurry. In the rush and confusion I followed several couples to the Truth Room and inside. The light was dim, and it seemed unlikely that I'd be spotted, though it appeared I was the only unaccompanied person here. Soon thirty or forty people were present.

There weren't any chairs or benches, just a carpet over the floor, and everybody sat cross-legged or sprawled on the carpet. I looked around, checking the room against Olive's and Randy's description of it. All the walls were draped with black cloth, but on the right were half a dozen wooden chairs by a door leading to the Healing Room. Up front was a small wooden rostrum, or speaker's stand; Trammel would speak from there.

About five minutes after I sat down on the carpet the basket was passed, and then Trammel came from somewhere in the rear and walked to the speaker's stand. He started to talk through a microphone on the stand, but speaking more quietly this time, and informed us that the message would occupy one hour, after which he would lead us in a Trammelite prayer before the lights came on again. As he spoke the lights dimmed until darkness was complete. Rheostatically controlled, I thought, probably from Trammel's rostrum.

Trammel continued, saying that tonight he would deliver a sermon on the moral danger of filth in literature. I grinned in the darkness as he quietly launched into an attack on Henry Miller. Henry Miller had to go, that was all there was to it, said Trammel, in much more mellifluous and specific words than those. I grinned again as he began reading, to prove his point that Miller had to go, a passage that I recalled first enjoying in "Tropic of Cancer." Either Trammel was reading from a Braille edition, or he'd memorized it.

I'd heard enough, and moved toward the entrance. Nobody stopped me as I went outside, and that seemed logical, because probably on several occasions people had left the Truth Room before the sermon had ended, having received enough truth to fix them good. I walked alongside the building toward Trammel's house, digging from my coat pocket a small flashlight Hunt had given me.

As I walked close to the building's wall, I could hear Trammel's voice, faint but still hot stuff; then it faded behind me as I reached his house. In half a minute I'd got the door open and stepped inside. I heard a noise from somewhere ahead of me in the house. Moving quietly, I crossed the room to a closed door which opened into a darkened hallway; at its end a thin slice of light spilled from another room, and from inside it came the sounds.

I walked forward slowly, as quietly as I could, hearing a man's voice, but unable to distinguish the words. The door was open about six inches, and when I reached it and leaned against the wall, by looking through the crack I could see into the room.

And there, mumbling to himself, was Arthur Trammel.

Chapter Fourteen

I SPRANG AWAY from the wall as if the old buzzard had spat tobacco juice in my eye. For a moment I stood rigid in the hall's dimness, but then I eased my eye into position once more and took a good look.

One thing about Trammel was sure: Nobody else in this world, or the next one, looked like him. Anybody who even remotely resembled him had to be Arthur Trammel. And this mumbling egg in there had the squashed head, chummy eyeballs, bushy brows, and lascivious lips of the Leader. It was Arthur for sure.

Then I discovered that he wasn't mumbling in his chops, but was talking to another man, because the guy came into the range of my eye. It was the blind man. He was now, oddly enough, wearing glasses.

In the same way that a man might almost admire the biggest and most gruesome boil in the world, I almost admired Trammel. I tiptoed back to the front door, around to the Truth Room's entrance, and inside. I sort of felt my way through people, getting myself cursed a couple of times in ungodly fashion, but reached the wooden stand where Trammel was still speaking, giving Miller all kinds of hell.

There I flicked on my flashlight. In the brief moment before I completely shaded its glow—not that anybody was looking up here, anyway—I caught a startling glimpse of one of those creamy-white thighs Trammel had so recently been condemning. Of course, there was no sign of Trammel. If there had been, I'd no doubt have let out a yowl that would have caused a great commotion in the congregation, but all my flash revealed was the slowly unwinding spools of tape on an expensive tape recorder.

I turned off the flashlight and stood for a moment thinking that Trammel had his pitch honed down to a fine point, and that there were two reasons for dousing the lights. The other one being that for almost an hour, while he addressed these citizens, he could be resting in his house, taking a nap, or writing another speech if he felt like it. Or paying off blind men.

I meant to change all that, though. I nosed around the Truth Room a little longer, then went back to Trammel's house and waited for him and his hireling to leave, because I couldn't very well afford any hue and cry. The hour must have been almost ended when the front door opened and somebody came out.

I couldn't tell if it was one of the blind men or their Leader, but I followed him and watched him walk through the wall and into the Truth Room. That was certainly what it looked like; he walked up to the wall and right through it. But when I followed half a minute later I went through it, too, simply by parting one of the black drapes I'd earlier noticed lining the walls.

Standing inside, I heard another sound, a soft click, and then after the briefest pause Trammel's voice continued on only a slightly higher pitch. He was back; what I'd heard was him switching off the recorder. As he concluded his message and announced the final prayer, I went back through the wall and stood there holding the drape aside until the lights came up and I could definitely see Trammel. Then I walked to his house again.

It was empty this time. I went through the whole place fast, but in fifteen minutes I hadn't found anything important to me. The most interesting item was a box in the bedroom closet. It contained spools of tape for the recorder. Each of the spools bore a small sticker on which was written a notation of its message. That was understandable. It would be hell for Trammel to announce that his text for the evening would be "The Evil in Plunging Necklines," and accidentally come on with "Let's Ban People." Several spools were marked with an author's name, some bore titles of books I'd read, a few had subject titles.

In the room I'd first peeked into I checked the phone on Trammel's desk just to be sure it bore the Davenport number June had given me. It did. I looked at the phone for a couple of minutes, thinking, then dialed the operator. I went through the routine I'd used with June again, only since I was using Trammel's phone I told the operator I was Arthur Trammel.

"I think someone has been using my phone for long-distance calls, Operator," I told her. "In my absence. Would you let me know what calls were made from this phone Sunday?"

She didn't give me any trouble, and in another few

minutes I had a list of three calls. The one I was interested in was there; it almost had to be, the way this was shaping up. I dropped the phone onto the hook and headed for confession—only there was going to be a new procedure in the Healing Room tonight. This time Trammel would do the confessing.

In the dimness of the Truth Room only one solitary figure sat. Shortly after I entered, an old man came out of the door beyond which was the hall leading to the Healing Room. The other person, a woman, went inside. When she came out, a few minutes later, I walked to the door. I would be the last to confess; maybe the last for quite a while.

The hall was about fifteen feet long, stretching down the right side of the building, and a closed door was at its end. As I took my first steps toward the closed door ahead of me I glanced around the hall, which was fairly well lighted. An odd note was a strip of mirror about head high, extending the hall's length, and for a moment it looked merely like a peculiar decoration. Then, all of a sudden, I remembered the one-way mirror I'd been using to peek at my neon tetras.

I ran toward that closed door and threw it open. The room was in darkness, but light spilled in behind me and I could see that the room was empty. Another door stood open on my left. I jumped through it in time to hear the sound of running feet and a man's voice shouting somewhere outside. Beyond the door, paralleling the hall down which I'd just walked and extending its length, ran another narrow hallway; light spilled in through the "mirror." I heard another shout.

The only way out of here that I was sure didn't wind up in a dead end was the way I'd come in. I sprinted back that way, down the hall, and into the Truth Room, made one big jump toward the exit, and stopped, skidding. Arthur Trammel came flying through the door and yelled, "There he is!" and two guys materialized beside him, and one of them yanked up a gun and there was a deafening noise as he pulled the trigger.

There were a lot of reflexes inside me almost simultaneously. A slug snapped past my head and I ducked, my hand automatically going to my armpit, where there was nothing but armpit. I realized that I was *not* carrying a gun, that both the other guys were because now I could see two guns, that they both wore police uniforms, and that I was sunk. There was no way for me to get out of here except by running past the cops and off into the hills with ten or twelve bullets in me.

That whole swarm of impressions took about a tenth of a second, and then I was spinning around to run. I guess I thought I'd just run until I banged into a wall somewhere, but then came inspiration, and it was Trammel who had given it to me—when he'd walked through the wall. I was already running, so all I had to do was to keep going and aim a couple of yards to the left, where I hoped nothing but drape was, and run faster. I hit the cloth and went literally ripping through it and outside as a few more wild shots cracked behind me.

I swung left and sprinted toward the revival tent, in dim light from the building behind me for a few seconds and then in darkness, but there was one hell of a lot of shouting by now, not just from the men I'd seen, but from what sounded like a small army. Feet were slapping all over the place as people ran toward the spot where those shots had been fired, and light blazed in my face moments before a man's deep voice yelled something and he and the light plunged toward me. I dropped my legs from under me and went down toward where I hoped his knees were, angling sideways with my shoulder thrusting forward, like a halfback taking out the enemy end, and his knees were there.

He went over me roaring. I scraped up a lot of dirt with my left shoulder and the side of my face, but I didn't go back to kick the guy, just rolled over and onto my feet and kept running. All I could hear was yelling and feet traveling over the ground, but nobody was shooting. I reached the tent and ran inside and up to the edge of the stage, with my flashlight on and sweeping around till I spotted Trammel's chest mike. I grabbed it and the coil of cord and sprinted back outside, hoping the wire didn't catch on anything and hoping most of all that this damn mike worked when I pressed the button.

I let the cord run out behind me until I figured I'd used most of it, then I flopped onto the ground in darkness. Even this far from Trammel's tent, there were a couple of guys with flashlights roaming around. Lying quietly, I could hear a guy behind me running; then he stopped ten yards or so away. He just stood there.

The two people with flashlights didn't worry me at the moment; they were far enough away. The guy near me might be trouble, though. But I couldn't wait any longer, so I pressed down the switch on the microphone in my hand, put my lips close to it, and said softly, "Hey."

A hundred feet or more away from me, back inside the tent, where the speakers were, I said, "Hey." Trammel wasn't the only foxy bastard. Knowing the mike was working, I strangled at about half volume into the mike: "Hey! Here he is, here's the bastard—*a-a-a-ah-h!*"

It went rolling over the hills like thunder. But it obviously came out of the tent, and I could see lights converging on it, hear a sudden uprush of yells. The guy who had been standing ten yards away came toward me saying, with no originality, "Hey! Hey!" And as he loomed before me I loomed up off the ground and all over him.

He got my left hand, knuckles sticking straight out like blunt knives, in his solar plexus, but what really finished him was the microphone on his skull and the edge of my palm in his throat. There was an ugly sound inside the tent, where there had already been so many ugly sounds, and the guy I'd slugged went down.

I went down with him. The two flashlights were bobbing toward us, and I got my knees under me in case I had to go through this again. But the men went past twenty feet away, close together, and raced toward the tent, where there was now a great deal of commotion. I even heard two closely spaced gunshots, but by then I was going like a rabbit away from everybody.

With my lungs still aching from that wild race through trees and over hills, because I had run a long time before slowing down, I walked up the last hill.

At its top I walked ahead to the clearing where Nurse Dixon was buried. My shovel still was there. I didn't spend any time looking for another grave; in that long walk I'd remembered something that hadn't impressed me at the time it had happened. When I'd followed Wolfe here, I'd found the grave he'd just filled—found it by stepping in its soft earth, feeling my shoe sink into it; but when I'd seen it for the second time I had seen the smooth and level surface of the grave, with no imprint in it at all, no indentation.

So now in the light from my flash I merely glanced around the small clearing, then started digging. I pulled the late Miss Dixon from the ground, rolled her a yard away, then dug deeper. When I struck something yielding I threw the shovel from me, scraped dirt away with my

87

hands, then grasped the small, cold shoulders in my fingers and pulled her from the ground.

And, this time, it was Felicity.

Chapter Fifteen

I DON'T KNOW how long I stayed there with what remained of Felicity Gifford. And an hour later I wouldn't even know for sure what I'd thought during those first minutes. But I must have remembered everything her friends had said about her in these last two days, remembered what her room had been like, how drab her clothes had been. I know I remembered that she'd been sixteen years old.

I brushed the dirt from her face, and it was quite a bit like the face in that portrait of her I'd seen. I looked at her for a long time. You can't hurt the dead, I know, by what you say about them or do to what's left of them, so when I'd finished lowering Felicity into the grave again I was suddenly surprised, and a little confused, remembering the exaggerated care with which I'd handled her body.

I balled up my fist and started to slam it against my other hand, then stopped and walked to Miss Dixon instead, dropped her into the grave, and shoveled dirt in on both of them.

Only one small bulb burned at the entrance to Greenhaven's parking lot, half a block from the wall around the building itself, and there wasn't an attendant present. I was sweating. Twice I'd had to duck out of sight as police cars passed me on the street, and every time I heard a siren I shivered.

Arthur Trammel, now that I'd eyeballed him through his one-way mirror and latched onto his mike, would know I was onto his tricks. My charging out of his hidden entrance to the Truth Room would tell him I'd seen him use it and must be aware of his tape-recorded deception. He'd have called all the cops in all the counties, and there'd be even more prowl cars hunting me now.

A few cars were in the lot and I found an unlocked

gray club coupé, a Chrysler convertible with the top up, and the name Lynette Nichols on its registration slip. I climbed in back and waited for her.

When I saw her walking diagonally across the lot I didn't know it was Lyn at first because she was wearing a tan-colored suit instead of the white uniform. But then I saw her face in the dim light, recognized her, and ducked down out of sight.

Her feet scraped on gravel and I heard her humming softly, then she got into the car and slammed the door shut. She must have heard me rising up behind her because she started to gasp, but I pressed my right hand over her mouth, left hand gripping her shoulder so that she couldn't get away.

She lunged against my hand, but I said rapidly, "I'm not going to hurt you. I've got to talk to you, that's all. I won't hurt you."

She held herself motionless, body tense.

"This is the only way I could get near you, get to talk with you, and it's important. This is Shell Scott. But I'm not crazy, and I've got to convince you of that first. I had to be sure you couldn't scream or run. Understand?"

After a few seconds she relaxed and nodded her head, lips soft against my palm. I said, "I'm going to let you go. Just don't scream." I paused, then added, "I tried to tell you last night that Dr. Wolfe and Nurse Dixon were performing abortions here at Greenhaven. Well, they were, and they killed a girl yesterday."

I took my hand away. For a moment she didn't move, then slowly her head turned and her wide dark eyes stared at me. Her lips were parted, her breathing was heavy. I said softly, "Don't be frightened. I just need some help."

She moistened her lips and finally spoke. "I—I won't scream. Give me a moment, Mr. Scott."

"Take as long as you want."

She was turned in the front seat, still breathing heavily, looking directly at me. In the dim light, with soft shadows on her face, she seemed even lovelier than when I'd seen her before. Finally she swallowed and tried to smile. "I don't imagine I could run if I wanted to. You might as well sit up front."

I climbed over the seat.

She asked slowly, "What was that about a girl being killed?"

"Just what I said."

"You mean a girl died at Greenhaven after an abortion?"

"A sweet little gal named Felicity Gifford, the one I asked you about Sunday night. And she came here for an abortion, all right, but that's not what killed her. She was murdered."

Lyn gasped and was quiet for seconds. "Murdered?" she said finally.

"With cyanide. I just got through taking a long look at her, and if you've ever seen anybody dead from potassium cyanide, you know what they look like. I've seen half a dozen before this, and that's what killed her. I'm here now because I need information from somebody familiar with Greenhaven—preferably you. Neither Wolfe nor Dixon can do any talking. They're both dead."

She gasped. "Both . . . Why do you say *she's* dead?"

"I dug up her body a couple of times. Don't jump to conclusions. I didn't kill her. I think a guy named Arthur Trammel killed her."

She moistened her lips, staring at me, then swallowed again.

I said, "Let me ask you a question, and please give me an honest answer. Do you think I'm enjoying a brief period when I talk rationally and seem normal, or do you think maybe I've been sane all along?" She started to speak and I broke in. "Wait a minute. Give me an honest answer. If you're afraid that any minute now I'll start giggling and snorting, and change from Dr. Jekyll into Mr. Hyde, I know you won't listen very closely to what I'll be saying."

"I'll tell you the truth, Mr. Scott."

"Shell. Am I nuts?"

"I'm really not sure, Mr.—Shell." She looked at me steadily. "Now let me ask some questions."

"O.K., if you make them fast."

"Why fast?"

"If a cop wanders in here and spots me, he'll shoot me."

"Oh." She frowned. "They've been patrolling around here all night. All right, fast. One, what would you do if I got out of the car?"

"Start running."

"After me?"

"Nope. Just running like a fool, fast and far. If you take off, there'll be little point in my sticking around."

"Two, why did you attack the police officers?"

"If I'm goofy, it was a whim; if I'm not, you've enough sense to answer that one yourself." I grinned at her.

"Besides, I'll bet you didn't feel much sympathy for those eggs; I gave Sergeant Meadows a pop for you."

She smiled. This was going very well, I thought. She had about the nicest smile I'd ever seen. Even nicer than Jo's. "Three," she said, "do you really expect me to believe Dr. Wolfe was going to kill you?"

"That hypo was loaded. If somebody—Dixon, eight to five—squirted the stuff out and stuck the hypo back into its case in a hurry—which I'm sure is what happened, since she was undoubtedly right outside Wolfe's door—there'll still be traces in the barrel. Enough to analyze, anyway. If it isn't some kind of poison, I give up. And I'll bet it's potassium cyanide."

The next question came more slowly. "You just said you think Arthur Trammel killed Miss Dixon. He's an important man, respected—"

"Not by me."

"—well known. Can you prove it?" She was looking intently at my face.

I told her the truth. "Nope. Not yet. If we had time I could list about ten points one after another, after which I think you'd be convinced. Right now I don't have the time. Well, want me to look at ink blots?"

She took a deep breath, let it out. "No."

"Now the big question: Can we get out of here? A little farther away from all the cops?"

She turned the key in the ignition. "Sit on the floor." I slid down to the floor boards as she drove out to the street and turned left. A few minutes later Lyn parked and said, "We can either talk in the car or go in there." She pointed out the window past me at a place called Terry's. "It's a little bar, but there usually aren't many people here."

"Let's go in."

Terry's was empty except for a bartender and a man and woman at the bar. Lyn and I slid into one of the booths, which was lighted by a candle, and I blew the candle out. Without a flashlight or remarkable eyes, anybody would have trouble spotting me as Shell Scott—particularly in my funereal garb. We got a bourbon and water for me, a Scotch and soda for her, and I began talking, starting clear back when I'd begun looking for Felicity. Every once in a while Lyn interrupted with what I thought of as ink-blot questions.

At one point she said, "The girl was at Greenhaven all day?"

"All day long. She got the phone call Saturday night and probably left right afterward—certainly sometime before daylight. Incidentally, was Dixon always on duty from midnight on? And how about Wolfe?"

"He was surgeon in charge of the hospital, and on twenty-four-hour call, but he worked days mostly. Dixon was on from midnight till eight."

"Just right. They could perform the operations between midnight and eight A.M., when nobody else was roaming around, and the girl could leave during those same hours the next morning. All very careful, safe, professional. Only Felicity didn't make it." I paused for a moment, then went on. "The operation would have been between midnight and eight Sunday morning. They killed her around noon."

Lyn shuddered. "You can't know when she died."

"Close enough. Don't forget, I saw her carried away by Wolfe. And rigor mortis was complete." I thought of how strange that shadow had appeared to me when I'd been crouched near the back door at Greenhaven and had seen the figure of a man surmounted by a rigid something, the shadow oddly like the letter T. The rigid form had been Felicity's body.

I explained to Lyn, then said, "At least, she'd been dead a good many hours, and Wolfe had to wait until night before he could safely carry her away and bury her. They probably had her body hidden in a locked room all afternoon. You can imagine how jittery they were. And then what happened? Me. I happened."

Lyn nodded slowly, a faint frown wrinkle between her eyes, soft highlights the color of amber glinting in her hair.

I said, "When I hit Greenhaven last night and you hauled that guy, your impersonator, away, you stopped and talked to Wolfe in the hall. He told me you'd mentioned something to him about my looking for Felicity." She nodded. "He came down and sounded me out with some phony chatter, just to make sure, then took off. Right after that I got slugged and wound up in a strait jacket. He could hardly let me keep nosing around. I told Wolfe myself that I was looking for Felicity Gifford. I'm surprised he didn't keel over. He knew I wasn't babbling, or off my rocker." I shrugged. "Exit Shell Scott."

She pressed her lips together and the frown deepened. This was a lot for her to get hit with all at once. "Why in the world would he use a knife, or whatever it was?" she asked. "That's so obvious."

"No matter what method he used, it would obviously have been murder. That's a pretty high emotional peak he'd have had to work up to, anyway. Why do people carry paper napkins out of burning houses? Besides, a prowl car arrived as I was leaving; who called the cops?"

"I did."

"I thought so. There were two calls to the Raleigh police from your office. I suppose Wolfe knew they were on their way?"

"Yes, I told him and the others I was going to phone."

"So there's the big reason: Wolfe had to finish me off in one hell of a hurry, if at all. Well, it was close. I'd barely got out of that strait jacket when the cops arrived."

"That's how we learned you were gone, when the police came in. The strait jacket wasn't in the room, though, and you said you didn't take it."

"All I took was a scar on my back. I figure Wolfe must have peeked in on me again, just before the cops arrived, and learned I had dissolved. He probably took out the strait jacket. It was cut and had bloodstains on it, which would have made my story sound pretty sane."

"I suppose. It looked to us as if you'd vanished, jacket and all. You can imagine how puzzled everybody was."

"Yeah, everybody except Wolfe. Uh, how'm I doing?" She smiled. "Pretty well."

Getting a smile like that one meant I was doing very well. I said, "Just one more point and I'll shut up. Do you know what time I was stuck into that room? In my strait jacket? I think I remember, but I want to be sure."

"It's all in the records. I went over them tonight. We took you into the room at about twenty-five after nine. Your escape was discovered at nine-forty-two."

I reached into my pocket for the slip of paper on which I'd written the four phone calls out of Greenhaven, slid it across the table to Lyn. "Wolfe phoned out at nine-sixteen and again at nine-forty. Seems odd that he'd phone the same guy just before those goons jumped me and also right after he'd tried to kill me and messed it up. I don't think that's a coincidence any more than the fact that both Dixon and Felicity were in the same grave. And Wolfe phoned Trammel."

She studied the paper for a few seconds, then squinted at me, cocking her head slightly on one side, thick red hair tumbling down onto her shoulder.

"That's not all," I said. "I found out tonight that Arthur

93

Trammel put in a call to Wolfe's phone at Greenhaven on Sunday. The time was just a few minutes after noon. So that's when he told Wolfe to kill Felicity."

She shook her head back and forth slowly. "I don't understand."

"You're getting all these little things at once, but think about it a minute and you'll put them together. I've had plenty of time to think about it, and they fit—one way. There's only one answer. Trammel got Felicity pregnant."

Chapter Sixteen

It didn't take long after that to convince Lyn that I was talking sense, and we cleaned up some tag ends. I said, "The time I estimated she'd been dead fits perfectly with the time of Trammel's phone call to Wolfe, too. What did Wolfe do when all the hue and cry started after my escape?"

"For a couple of hours after the police arrived, all of us were looking for you, searching the grounds and all the rooms. Dr. Wolfe and I weren't together, but policemen were with both of us. After all, you were . . . violent." She smiled.

"You searched all the rooms? Felicity must still have been there somewhere."

"Dr. Wolfe would undoubtedly have had the girl in a room of the hospital ward, since he's in charge of it," she said. "And we all searched our own areas with the police. I looked through the east wing, where my office is. He'd probably have put her in a bed, as if she were sleeping. And nobody was looking for a girl, anyway. We were all looking for a great big maniac."

"And I got back to Greenhaven just in time to see Wolfe hauling the body away. That would have been his big worry, naturally. After that he'd have had to remove any evidence that she'd been there." I thought of something then. "Wolfe's search area was the hospital ward, huh? Where is that located in Greenhaven?"

"At the end of the west wing."

"He was coming from the west wing in a big hurry when I ran into him and we had our . . . difficulty."

We sat quietly for a little while, then I asked her, "Still think I'm nuts?"

"Yes, I do." She smiled. "But a harmless nut." Lyn shook her head. "You did act pretty crazy, though, pretty crazy."

From then on we forgot the case, started getting acquainted. It was as though there'd been a signal and it was time to relax. We had a few more drinks, talking cozily like old friends.

We were gurgling happily when the bartender said, "Last call for drinks," and it was nearly two A.M.

"Where in the world did the time go?" she asked.

"I don't know. But I'll bet it went to a happy place."

"You're fun, Shell." She looked at me for a long second, then said quietly, "We'd better go."

Outside I held the car door while she scooted in, then I slammed it and said, "I'll call you at Greenhaven, Lyn. It would help if you could check with those two guards and find out for sure who sapped me. And there might be something—"

"Shell, I know you can't have any place to stay."

"Oh, yes, I do. I've got a dandy little fox burrow where I snuggle up. Dispossessed the hermit. He was a foxy character."

"Come home with me. I'd like to help you, Shell. I helped put you in this mess. And now I know you're just a little crazy. I can't let you sleep in your—fox burrow."

"Well . . ."

"Don't act so shocked, either."

"I'm not shocked."

"I mean, I've got a couch in the front room."

"Ah, the psychoanalytic couch."

"Sure. I'm going to psychoanalyze you. Besides, I want to laugh some more. Get in, Shell—just for laughs."

"Just for laughs," I said, and I got in.

Lyn took our coffee cups into the kitchen. We had spent half an hour here in her apartment talking about the case and I'd told her the things she might look for at Greenhaven tomorrow. When she came back into the living room, she said, "We might as well go to bed."

It may have been some indication of the way this little tomato was beginning to affect me, since those words went through me like a short circuit through bath water. I sprang to my feet. "Might as well!"

95

You would think I'd never even heard of a gal named Jo Perrine. Lyn smiled, then composed her face and walked into the bedroom, and on her way back out almost collided with me. She was carrying a pillow, sheets, and two blankets, which she dropped on a small, lumpy couch.

"There you are," she said.

"No," I said, grinning at her from the bedroom door. "Here I am."

She proceeded briskly to fix a bed on the couch, called me over, and sat me down on it. "Good night, Shell."

"You sleepy?"

"Ho, ho," she said, and went into the bedroom, and I could hear her preparing for sleep, moving about, rustling and what not, and if you want the whole truth, those sounds disturbed me enormously. Despite my sly queries, like "Sure you don't need these blankets?" and "You don't feel like dancing, do you?" she kept on moving about and humming.

Then her light went out, and bedsprings squeaked. The sound of bedsprings squeaking means nothing all by itself; the squeaks have to be connected in your mind with whoever or whatever is going on before the noise has real significance. If there had somehow been, for example, an old housebroken horse in there, I wouldn't have given those squeaks a second thought. But I *knew* there was no horse in there.

Well, I lay awake quite a while, but when I finally did fall asleep my dreams were sensational.

I woke up with a sore back and a stiff neck, but with a feeling that all was well with the world. In a few minutes I remembered that all was not exactly well, but I still felt good enough.

Lyn was bustling about in the kitchen, humming merrily. In a minute she came out into the front room. "Hi," she said. "How did you sleep?"

"I don't know myself how I managed it, but I did get a wink or two."

She winked at me. "That makes three, and don't get smart. Get up instead before I pull the covers off you."

"This is a test: I'm not getting up."

"And I'm not pulling the covers off. What do you want for breakfast?"

"Coffee. And toast. That's all."

She shook her head, went back into the kitchen, and closed the door. I got up and dressed.

Over a second cup of coffee she said, "I'd stay here, Shell, but it might look funny if I didn't go to Greenhaven. Have you thought of anything else I could do?"

"We've covered it all, I think."

"Want me to phone you here? I'll be back for lunch."

"That's soon enough."

"What are you going to do, Shell?"

"Just sit. I've got plenty to think about. And for God's sake, you be careful. Don't give anybody an idea of what you're doing. If Trammel's all I think he is, he'd kill half the population to keep it from getting out."

She finished her coffee and got up. "Well, 'by."

I walked to the front door with her and said, "Lyn, be damned careful. Remember, as far as you're concerned, whoever you talk to, Shell Scott is a raving maniac."

She left. I hadn't realized the apartment would seem so empty.

After a while I went to the phone, looked up Mrs. Gifford's number, and dialed. It was a short conversation. I told her as gently as I could, but the fact of death can never be stated gently. She shrieked and wailed over the sound of the TV blaring in the room behind her, and I explained that Felicity was really dead, that she'd been dead more than a day when I found her body. Before I could finish, she hung up on me. I hadn't even told her that her daughter had left Saturday night for an abortion; I doubt that Mrs. Gifford would have believed me, in any event.

I was aware that my name was synonymous by now with homicidal insanity, but I'd got the impression that Mrs. Gifford had been afraid even to talk to me over the phone. I wondered how many other L.A. citizens felt the same way about me. By noon I had a rough idea. By noon I'd read the morning paper that was delivered at Lyn's door, and listened to enough news broadcasts so that I knew how deep the hole I was in had become.

It was worse than I'd thought it would be. Everybody seemed to have taken it for granted that I had suddenly and actually gone insane, murdered Wolfe at Greenhaven, and overpowered a police force. There wasn't a word in type or speech that intimated that I might be the victim of circumstances or a frame. This was open and shut, and I gathered that all the cops for miles around, plus a good number of panting citizens, were looking for me.

I could thank Arthur Trammel and his Guardians for one new development that helped not at all. The morning paper carried Trammel's remarks on the front page. He stated that I had, after escaping from Greenhaven and remaining under cover throughout the day, cornered him in the room where he held his confessional and attempted to murder him. After describing his miraculous escape from death, much distorted with soap-opera phrases such as "Scott's bulging, red-flecked eyes," he declared that simply because he, Trammel, had denounced the madman from the pulpit and in the press, I had sneaked up on him and tried to knock him off. I'd murdered before and last night had tried again; I must be found and destroyed; and so on. Corroboration of his story was supplied, naturally, by all six of the other Guardians.

Shortly after noon Lyn's key turned in the lock and she came inside. The room brightened considerably.

"Hi," she said. "How's my crazy man?"

"O.K. Missed you. Did you learn anything?"

"A little. Come on into the kitchen while I fix lunch, Shell. I want to get back around one."

I followed her into the compact, gleaming kitchen and she buzzed around dropping things into a pressure cooker while we talked. She'd been pretty busy at Greenhaven, and though she hadn't come up with anything that surprised me, she had got corroboration of several things I'd already been sure of in my own mind. She'd talked to the guards I'd put into Greenhaven's hospital and they admitted it was Wolfe who had told them I was a violent nut and that they were to "subdue" me; he'd been the boy who'd sapped me from behind.

Lyn had found no evidence that Wolfe and Dixon had been performing abortions, but I hadn't expected her to, since, after killing Felicity, they'd have made sure there wasn't any around. Lyn had, however, arranged for a test to be run on the residue in Wolfe's syringe. It was potassium cyanide.

I said, "That just about wraps it up. You got a lot done, Lyn."

She frowned. "It doesn't wrap up Trammel. How are you ever going to find out for sure about him?"

I grinned at her. "The logical way. Ask him."

98

Her mouth dropped open. "*Ask* him! You don't mean you're going down there tonight—"

"No. Not tonight. No meeting tonight. And for what I've got in mind, the meeting has to be in full swing, which it will be tomorrow. And I didn't say I was going to ask him politely." She looked pretty flabbergasted and I changed the subject. "You have any trouble this morning?"

"No, but . . . a few more policemen talked to me."

"What did you tell them?"

"You're a schizo, and real gone. Big menace, Scott."

"Good. You're sure?"

"I told you I'd do it your way. But . . ." She frowned. "There was a kind of bad break."

She had talked to a reporter who knew that Nurse Dixon had disappeared the same night I'd shot Wolfe and escaped. The reporter had learned from the police that I'd "admitted" having seen the nurse just before I'd plugged Wolfe. He had asked Lyn if it wasn't a reasonable assumption that I might have "killed the nurse because she was a witness to his murder of Wolfe."

Lyn said to me, "I had to tell him it was a possibility."

"Sure, honey. He'd probably have written it that way, anyway, as having come from an authoritative source. The only difference is that now he can quote you."

That was true enough, but I could imagine the upcoming story: "A lovely young Greenhaven nurse, Gladys Dixon, may have been a second victim of the insane killer Sheldon Scott, it was alleged today by Dr. L. Nichols, Greenhaven's chief psychiatrist. Miss Dixon, a young, glamorous, exciting, shapely, sultry, etc., etc."

She said, "Have you seen the paper?" I nodded. She walked to me and put her hands on my chest. "Shell, wouldn't it help if I did come right out and say I knew you were sane, normal—no matter what you've actually done? *Everybody's* against you. Pretty soon you won't be able to stop it, won't be able to convince a soul."

I squeezed her hands and said, "No, thanks, Lyn. We settled that, and it's bad enough that I'm here, sticking your neck out. Nobody would hear you now, anyway; your word would be one against an encyclopedia. If this deal ever reaches court, I can use all the high-powered steam you can generate—but not till I say so, and certainly not while Trammel's loose. But thanks."

In almost no time she was taking pork chops, potatoes, and carrots out of the pressure cooker. The food was so good we didn't let conversation interfere with our enjoyment of it, so it was fairly quiet until we finished. This Lyn was a woman a guy could enjoy twenty-four hours a day. She didn't find it necessary to chatter all the time; she didn't mind silences. I liked looking at her, talking to her, and just knowing she was around even when I couldn't see her.

A little before one, Lyn said, "Well, 'by. See you about three."

"Three? I thought you were going to work."

"I am, but I'll be back." She smiled. "This morning, oddly enough, I developed a splitting headache. I'm sure nobody will expect me to last the day."

"Clever. You're too fast for me."

"Aren't I?" She got up and walked to the front door.

"Wait a minute," I said. "That's *too* fast."

"Ho, ho." The door closed and she was gone.

Those two hours from one till three were a long, dull afternoon, and when Lyn returned it was a short happy afternoon and evening. Until around eight P.M.

We got it first on a broadcast, then Lyn went out and bought a late paper and we went over it together. I assumed Mrs. Gifford must have called the cops and that a reporter picked it up from there. It was now common knowledge that I'd informed Mrs. Gifford that her daughter was dead. Most of the rough stuff was between the lines—I might have killed the girl myself, I might merely have been indulging in some heavy sadism directed at the girl's mother. The statement that made up my mind, though, was a quote from Lieutenant French of L.A.'s Missing Persons Bureau; who noted, sensibly enough, that there wasn't even proof yet that the girl was dead; that no body had been found.

I said to Lyn, "Looks like I've got to leave the apartment tonight after all."

"Shell, I don't want you to, and you don't have to."

"I'm not crazy about going out, myself. But I mean to phone French, and I'm not going to phone from here. The main reason I didn't tell the cops about Dixon and Felicity and that grave before now was for fear word would fly around that I'd killed both of them. If they'd dug up Felicity they'd have found Dixon first—and I'm stuck with a damned good motive for killing Dixon. But, hell, it's flying all over anyway. And maybe this will pull me a little way out of the hole."

Half an hour later I was in a phone booth several miles from Lyn's apartment waiting for French to come on the line. Lyn had insisted on driving me and was in her Chrysler half a block away. When French answered I told him I was calling about his statement in the papers and he got interested all of a sudden. When I told him I knew where he could find Felicity's body there were two or three seconds of complete silence, then he said, "Who is this?"

"I'll tell you if you let me spill the rest of it fast—and forget about tracing the call. I'll be long gone, anyway."

After a short silence he said, "All right."

"This is Shell Scott." In fast, short sentences I told him that Wolfe and Dixon had killed Felicity, that I'd followed Wolfe and found the grave. "You'll find both Dixon and Felicity in it," I said, "but I didn't kill either of them. Cyanide killed the girl, but your autopsy will show she had an abortion. No matter what else I'm accused of, nobody can stick me with that, so find her and chalk me off—and do it out loud."

"Where are they?"

I told him, and it took too damned long to tell. I wanted off the line and far from this phone—especially with Lyn so close. I said, "You can get the parts I don't have time to tell from Sergeant Meadows and his sidekick, patrolman Al something, on the Raleigh force. And you can get all of it from the guy who sent Felicity to Wolfe and Dixon, Arthur Trammel—the guy who got Felicity pregnant in the first place. He murdered Dixon so there'd be nobody left to spill the beans about him."

I hung up and ran to the car and Lyn gunned the motor. All the way back to the apartment I kept thinking about what I'd said to French, particularly the bit about Trammel. There hadn't been time to explain to French all the little things that made me sure I was right. I told myself that I couldn't be wrong, that I had to be right, but there was still a fragment of doubt in my mind.

The next morning, in Lyn's apartment, we learned that a police crew had gone to the location I'd described, walked up to the top of that hill, and found nothing. No bodies. Just a soft, filled-in spot that might once have been a grave.

After the first shock, that made me feel pretty good. Finally I was sure about Trammel.

Chapter Seventeen

THERE WAS LESS than an hour of sunlight left when I flopped on my stomach on a high rise of land overlooking Trammelite headquarters. I wore my dark clothes, hat, and raincoat.

It was late Wednesday afternoon, and I'd left Lyn half an hour earlier. She'd driven me to within a mile of here and then returned home—after vainly pleading with me not to go through with my plan and get killed. I had informed her, truthfully, that there was no other plan available, and that I would be very careful not to get killed.

That had been in the car, about a minute before I'd climbed out, and Lyn had suddenly scooted toward me, put her arms around my neck, and kissed me. Her lips had been warm, soft, and hungry; and there must have been more than sixty seconds in that minute, so many things happened. If she hadn't taken her arms away and pushed me, telling me to go on and do whatever I was going to do, I'd never have left; it would never have occurred to me to leave.

My plan was simple: I was going to kidnap Arthur Trammel. Or maybe it was I that was simple. Beyond Trammel's house, between the low black Truth Room and the tent, dust swirled, and the delayed sound of an explosion reached my ears. The boys were still blasting to enlarge the Eternal House. I could see a dozen workmen moving around, but I had also spotted several other guys, in suits, who didn't seem to be working anything except their eyes, and who would probably object to my kidnaping the All-High.

But there was only one man alive who could clear me, and that man was Arthur Trammel. I hadn't the slightest doubt now that it *was* Trammel. As soon as I'd thought of him as the man responsible for Felicity's pregnancy and death, too many things, even aside from those I'd told Lyn about at Greenhaven and Terry's that night, fitted like pieces of a jigsaw puzzle: Trammel's flipping Sunday at that Guardian meeting, and especially the timing of his flip immediately after I'd mentioned Dixon's name; his needling me then until I'd flipped a little myself, and his continuing to ride me in the papers. It even explained why both Felicity's and Dixon's bodies had been in the same grave; and I thought I knew now why I hadn't caught Wolfe that first night when I'd followed him.

Trammel had probably ordered Felicity's murder without thinking twice about it, because of all the men in L.A., he was probably the one man who could least afford exposure of what he really was. If word got around that he was lusting for his young followers, taking advantage of their youth and ignorance to seduce them, practicing the exact opposite of what he preached, he'd fall from Master to monkey overnight and all his loyal Trammelites would feel like spitting on him, just as I did.

Felicity couldn't have been the only one; there must have been plenty of others—like Betha Green, maybe, I thought. Aside from all the other good reasons I had for wanting to get my hands on him, nobody else would know the story he could tell, certainly not all of it. Those missing bodies, for example—Trammel would have moved them himself to a safer spot. But with any luck, tonight I'd find out where they were buried, find out everything. All I had to do was ask him, in the right way.

That was all—just walk down there and kidnap him and then disappear into thin air. Down at the incomplete Eternal House dust swirled again from another explosion and a second later its dull booming sound reached me. As dust settled there was a sudden flurry of activity among the men. One guy waved his arms. Everybody raced away from the area except the arm-waver and one other guy, who ran up to the mouth of the hole that had been blasted in the cliff and charged about in silly fashion.

I looked at Trammel's house and the area around it. There wasn't much sunlight left and I had to plan my approach while I could still see the grounds clearly. Getting in there and out again wouldn't be any picnic, I knew, but I was looking forward to starting, looking forward to it and itching to get my hands on Trammel. In fifteen minutes more I'd picked my route and everything was settled; there was nothing to do but wait, think about Trammel and Lyn, and itch for both reasons.

I sat in the darkness of Trammel's front room, on the edge of a chair I'd placed before an open window. After dark, I'd waited on my belly near Trammel's house until he'd left it and walked to the Truth Room, waited another minute until the figure of a walking man was far enough away, then had run to Trammel's back door, torn the screen, and used a skeleton key to get in. There'd been no trouble yet, but it was nearly nine P.M., and the meeting would soon be over.

I could see half a dozen people on the grounds, their figures outlined by light spilling past the raised side of the tent where Trammel was speaking. I'd just watched him complete his standard tour through the crowd, ranting and raving, and now he was up on the stage concluding his address. Ordinarily everybody would have been inside at this time, and my guess was that those figures out there were guards.

The choral group began singing. It would be another ten minutes or so before Trammel would leave the Truth Room and come here to his house—if he repeated his actions of that night when I'd been here before—and the waiting already had me on edge. I wanted to get him, if I got him at all, after he left the Truth Room, because I had to start shaking his followers' faith in his magnificence, had to yank off the halo that Trammelites thought their Master wore.

The way most of them felt about him now, not even a confession from his own lips would shake their confidence and belief in him—unless that confidence and belief were already weakened. I couldn't think of any better way to start the weakening process than to have Trammel off in the hills somewhere, preferably with a few broken bones, when his tape-recorded spiel came to an end in the Truth Room.

Between the Truth Room, close by on my left, and the big tent, farther away, guard ropes were stretched before the mouth of the Eternal House; some "Danger" signs were stuck near them. One man stood about ten yards from the ropes; several other men were motionless farther away. As far as I knew, there was only one man behind this house, though, and I wasn't going to worry about him yet.

The singing stopped, lights came up outside and illuminated the grounds; organ music swelled gloomily in Trammel's theme song. I couldn't see the stage from which the All-High would now be descending, but I could see that the tent itself was jammed; recent publicity, and Monday night's "attack" on their Master, had brought out what might be a record crowd of Trammelites. I could see at least a thousand of them; the total might be three thousand or more.

Then Trammel stepped from the tent, and the tension that had been stretching for hours through my body seemed to concentrate in my stomach. I leaned forward, gripping the window sill tight as I stared at him. He walked with slow measured steps in time to the pulsing beat of the organ. When he was almost halfway to the Truth Room, walking parallel to the guard ropes, I forced myself to relax, stretched my fingers away from the window, feeling a tremor in my hands—and then all hell broke loose.

The earth seemed to heave out there in front of me, to shake and shudder in sudden sound and light. Almost in the middle of that violent sound and color, completely hidden in swirling clouds of smoke and dust, was—or had been—Trammel. For seconds I was partially blinded; then, on the fringe of that boiling cloud, I saw the man who had earlier been motionless there reel and fall. A rising wail came from his throat.

Dust began to settle, smoke rising into the air above it, and the former bright illumination seemed murky and thick after that shocking glare. There was silence then, a quietness accentuated by the speed with which it had followed that explosion and by the isolated whimpering sound of the man twisting slowly on the ground. And then there was a moan from the tent, from a thousand throats, a noise born in stunned shock and swelling in comprehension.

Movement flowed inside the tent. I saw figures pour slowly past the raised canvas, begin to run forward. Not even thinking about the chance that I might be seen and recognized, I slid through the window to the ground and ran toward the spot where Trammel and the other man lay.

A dozen men were there moments before me; beyond them the mass of the crowd had stopped running, pressed hesitantly closer. Silence had fallen again except for separate gasps or cries of horror as one or another came close enough to see—to see what I had already seen. There was nausea in my belly, numbness in my brain.

The man who had fallen got unaided to his feet, rising slowly, his cries silenced. Not looking at him, but at the focus of all other eyes, I still was aware of his suddenly arrested movement as he turned and saw what all of us had seen.

For Arthur Trammel was dead.

God, he was dead; not just lifeless, but horribly, shockingly, unbelievably torn and ugly, his body shattered, his blood staining the earth. I stood less than ten feet from him—from part of him.

He lay on his back. Blood smeared one side of his narrow face, but the other side was unmarked and almost obscenely white. The black robe he had worn was shredded, torn almost free of his thin body, and a red mass of torn flesh loomed on the side of his chest. Redness drained from it, slid down his side.

One arm was bent awkwardly beneath him, and the explosion's force had ripped his left leg from his body. The leg ended at his knee in a pulp of bone and cartilage and flesh; the bloody, unreal stump lay on the ground two yards from him, thick fluid oozing from both torn parts that seconds before had been one.

For a moment the only thing I could think of was that all my hopes, my chances, had died with Trammel; then, hoping that maybe, somehow, it wasn't he, I moved closer, stood above him, and looked down at the narrow face, tiny eyes staring blankly, his long hooked nose, at the uniquely ugly face of Arthur Trammel. It was unmistakably Trammel, and he was unmistakably dead.

A man raced up with a blanket, threw it over the still figure. The moaning began again. Across from me a woman cried out softly and slumped, someone's arms going about her and holding her off the ground. Those actions, the first quick movements in the few seconds I had stood here, brought me out of my own shock and I began backing away through the hundreds of others who had pressed near and were massed in a circle that had Trammel as its center. I was suddenly aware of the possibility that someone might recognize me. All eyes, though, were on the blanket-covered figure, and I pulled the hat lower on my forehead, raised the raincoat's collar to hide my face more completely.

Someone bumped into me and I swung around, but it was only a woman turning to push out of the crowd. Keeping my face down, I walked toward Trammel's house, breathed more easily when I reached the shadow at its side. Then somebody near me let out an exclamation, grabbed my arm.

I jerked my head around and in the dimness saw a square chunky man with big eyes in a red face, a Guardian, and he opened his mouth just in time for me to close it with an uppercut I didn't even know I'd started. His teeth clicked together and as he started to fall I sprinted into blackness. Yards farther, I looked back, but nobody was following me; the picture there was still the same, people edging away from the blanket-covered body.

For a while I walked without purpose or direction, wondering how the accident had happened—and then, slowly, I began wondering if it had been an accident. Plenty of people must have wanted Trammel dead. I remembered the sudden flurry of activity I'd seen this afternoon following one of the explosions. But it didn't make much difference to me now, one way or the other.

I kept walking until I found myself on residential streets, out of habit avoiding lights and hiding my face when I passed other men, and then I became aware that I was on a familiar street, before a familiar place. Automatically I had come back to Lyn.

Chapter Eighteen

LYN WAS WEARING a blue robe when she opened the door. Her face was sober, but when she saw me she smiled suddenly and said, "Shell, I was worried, so darn worried—" and then she was pressed close to me, her arms around my neck and her head moving against my chest.

In a moment she stepped back and looked at me, started to say something and stopped. I guess she could tell by my face that things had gone wrong, and she asked, "What happened?"

"Everything blew up. Literally. Hell with it." I tried on a grin. "Come back here. Wait, I'll go outside and knock and we'll try it again. Or maybe—"

"What do you mean, everything blew up?"

I told her. I told her the whole thing. We sat on that lumpy couch and she was quiet until I finished. Lyn knew all that I'd done until tonight, all I'd figured out, and she knew how much this night might have meant to me.

She said softly, "I'm sorry, Shell. Are you sure it was Trammel?"

"Yeah, baby, I'm positive. The light was dim, but everybody could see him well enough. His face wasn't messed up much more than usual, just one side. Besides, I walked up and practically stepped on him—and you know what old Squashhead looked like. Nobody could possibly mistake him for any other human being. For any human being, to tell the truth. Nope, Lyn, Trammel's *kaput*."

"What will you do now, Shell?"

"That's a good question."

I honestly didn't know what I could do now, and my mind was still a little dulled by the suddenness of what had happened. We sat on the couch, not talking, and I leaned back with my eyes closed. A minute later I felt Lyn's breath on my cheek, and after that her lips, soft, warm, and gentle.

I turned toward her and her lips slid over mine, still soft and warm, but in moments they were less gentle, more demanding. I slid my hands beneath her robe, against bare flesh; her skin felt hot under my fingers, and her flesh had the same liquid, yielding softness as her lips and tongue. I pulled her close, held her tight against me. There were soft noises deep in her throat and then, without opening her eyes, she spoke to me in a voice so low it was almost a whisper.

I lifted her, held her close against me, and walked toward the bedroom. Her mouth was still moist and parted, her eyes were still closed.

In the morning the sky was overcast and there was a chill in the air. You'd think I had enough to depress me without the weather's being gray and gloomy too. Still, I was nowhere near as low as I had been several hours earlier, for I was sitting on the couch, which, last night, I had not slept on.

Lyn was sitting on it, too. That is, in a way she was; I sat on the couch, and she sat on my lap. Those weren't the only reasons for my feeling better; the gal had a way with words, and a fine, logical mind, which she used like a woman part of the time, and like a psychiatrist part of the time. Both as woman and as psychiatrist she was terrific, and I was back to normal.

She said, "Look at the worst possible side of the mess, Shell. Even if everybody in the world believes terrible things about you, you know they're not true. And I know it, too."

"That's the best part. So what's next? Find an island, build a cabin, and get a fifty-year sunburn? Think of the fun we'd have peeling each other."

She smiled, dimples popping into delightful prominence in her cheeks. "Don't be silly. There must be something you can do. We *know* you're innocent, so there must be some way to prove it."

I grunted.

She slid off my lap, saying, "I'll fix us more coffee. You concentrate."

While she made noises in the kitchen I concentrated, with the usual result. As far as I was concerned, the outside world was on fire. I couldn't roam around, talk to people, ask questions, or even pop anybody on the head. The heat on me had been bad before, but it was really a fire now, an eighteen-alarm inferno. We'd read the morning papers and listened to the news broadcasts; all of them had the latest development.

The Guardians said I'd blown Trammel to pieces.

Nobody else said so, but my name was always mentioned, since the guy I'd slugged had passed word on that I was there; and though the possibility of an accident was admitted—since, as I'd guessed last night, there'd been some kind of peculiar misfire and some unbanged explosive could have been lying around—a bright six-month-old child might have guessed I'd done the buzzard in.

And the story—all of it, from my session with Trammel and the Guardians clear on up to last night's "tragedy"—had been picked up by the wire services today. Which was no great surprise to me. If there'd been pressure on the local police before, they were about to get squashed by it now.

Lyn came in carrying two cups of coffee. "Well, what have you figured out?"

I glared at her.

She grinned. "Look, you've been thinking too much about it. This is the psychiatrist speaking, sir. Get your mind off trouble for a while; let your subconscious work."

"O.K., psychiatrist. It will take more than my subconscious, plus my conscious and eight miracles, to get out of this one. But O.K., let's talk about you. I really don't know a hell of a lot about you. For one thing, how come such a sweet young lass is a psychiatrist at all?"

"Dad was a psychologist at Duke. I knew from the time I was so high that I wanted to be one, too, only more so. And I'm either blessed, or burdened, with a horribly retentive memory. Skipped a couple of early grades and did six years of college and pre-med in four. Then four years of medical school, two interning, and there you are. I was in private practice for a few months, then Greenhaven."

"Incidentally, what the devil goes on out there? Guys wandering around in the halls, strange things happening outside. *I* sure heard some strange things."

"Well, Greenhaven's a little different from most such places. We really don't have any homicidal cases—as you know now." She grinned. "Just the staff. There's the usual psychiatric treatment, but besides that, we stress personal honesty more than anything else."

I frowned at her. "What's that got to do with fixing up people in the shape I was supposed to be in?"

She grinned again. "We seldom get anybody as bad as you were supposed to be. And it's got more to do with mental health than you might think, Shell; it's the most important single thing, really. Without the technical talk, basically we almost force the patients to be honest with each other, and that's all it takes for a lot of them. They've all got so used to big or little dishonesties that it's difficult for most of them at first. But all by itself that improves their mental health surprisingly. Or maybe I shouldn't say surprisingly, since their dishonesties bother them whether they know it or not, give most of them their neuroses in the first place."

"I think I saw your process in operation." I told her about the two old hags and she laughed. I said, "And how many of your charges get their teeth knocked out?"

"None. Oh, it might not work in Podunk, but nobody gets too angry in Greenhaven because it's normal there. Everybody knows the others are just telling the truth as they see it, not making up nasty things to say." She dimpled. "It isn't like the world."

I got a big kick out of that. "Baby," I said, "can you imagine what the world would be if it were like that? A place where everybody *had* to be honest? No wars, no misunderstandings, no Communists, no Emily Posts, no jury trials—no detectives, even. You'd just ask a guy whodunit and he'd say, 'Me, I done it.'"

She clapped her hands. "Think of it! Advertisers would

110

say, 'This little pill won't cure ulcers or dandruff or any-thing. It's *worthless!*'" She squealed with laughter and I joined her.

Then suddenly I remembered who I was. "What the hell am I laughing at?"

"Oh, come on."

"I just happened to think. In your happy world, I wouldn't be in this mess. And Arthur Trammel would never have got started in the first place. Baby, I'll bet half the people in Greenhaven were put there by guys like that lying lecher."

"At least half."

"Maybe he's the price we pay for civilization. And you know what? It isn't worth it." I had some coffee. "I really like your honest world, honey. Just one little word and the walls would come tumbling down—including Greenhaven's. Maybe that's Utopia, Brave New World."

We had a lot of fun imagining ramifications of the Green-haven world, and then suddenly Lyn said, "Enough. Pre-tend you've got a client named Shell Scott. He's in an aw-ful jam, and you've got to unjam him."

I was quiet for a minute or two. "It's possible. Trouble is there's nothing to convict but a corpse."

"Well, convict the corpse. That would clear you."

"O.K. You and I are sure Trammel was playing around with lush little dolls, Trammelites who figured the Master couldn't do anything wrong if he tried. And we know he tried. So there must be other girls who could tell stories about Trammel and that healing hand of his."

"Do you think there might be others like—like Fe-licity?"

"There might even be other dead ones, but I kind of doubt it. Trammel never had a detective hot on his neck before. But I'll give ten to one Felicity wasn't the first girl he sent to Greenhaven."

"So all we have to do is find them."

"All *I* have to do—only it isn't quite that simple. After I find them I've got to get them talking. You'd have to know those Trammelites to realize how close-mouthed and adoring they are about that guy. And they'll probably be even more close-mouthed this soon after his death. There's thousands of them, too; be a job finding the right ones. You can bet Trammel was the only guy who knew all the names." I lit a cigarette and said, "I think I know one name, though: Betha Green."

111

I told her how Betha had acted and she said, "Think you'll talk to her again?"

"Yeah, but not right away. This damn town has to cool off a little first. Better if Trammel cools some more, too."

"Betha Green," Lyn repeated softly.

We spent a lazy morning and afternoon and about six o'clock I took a shower. When I came out Lyn was gone and a note said she'd be back in an hour or two. I almost walked a path in the carpet until I heard her key in the lock and she came inside.

"Where the hell have you been?" I asked her.

"I went to see Betha Green."

"Damn you, how many times—"

She walked up close to me and grinned. "It's done, so be sensible. Don't you want to hear what happened?"

I sputtered another minute, then said, "O.K. But I still damn you. Betha say anything?"

"Not a word. She was scared. I asked her about Trammel, Greenhaven, Dixon—all of it. She denied everything, but if I do say so, I'm a good psychiatrist. I'd take an oath she was lying."

"You shouldn't have gone, Lyn. Hell, you said yourself that if there's any place I'm safe it's here in the apartment of the psychiatrist who declared me nuts. So we can wait. And nothing came of it, anyway." I frowned at her. "What did you mean, she was scared? Because you talked to her?"

"No." Lyn pulled me over to the couch. As we sat down she said, "The funniest thing. She'd heard it and said all the Trammelites had heard it. I don't know whether Betha herself believed it or not."

"What are you talking about?"

"There's a rumor going around that Arthur Trammel will arise in three days."

Chapter Nineteen

THERE'S A WHAT?" I blinked at Lyn. "Who will arise? Not Trammel, baby. I wonder where the idea got started."

"Probably among the Trammelites themselves," Lyn said. "They all must be shocked by his death, and I imagine most of them want their leader back. Wishful thinking. Now that it's started, a lot of them will believe it'll happen—until they're disappointed."

"I suppose," I said. "Hope springs eternal in the human beast. But I wonder how the rumor got started. . . ." I stopped, and after a while I grinned at Lyn. "Hell, what do you bet," I said, "that Trammel *does* arise?"

This time she blinked at me.

"Baby, I think you called this one dead wrong," I said. "Those anxious Trammelites aren't going to be disappointed. It won't be Arthur, not unless they put him back together first, but it will be *a* Trammel—and it will still be good old All-High Arthur to the flock."

She kept frowning, then smiled at me. "I'm supposed to be the psychologist."

"Now we're even. I'm supposed to be the detective. But this might be just what I want. It's too good for the remaining Guardians to pass up. It's made to order. Trammelism is a big operation, profitable, getting powerful, but without Trammel himself it's just another cult. If the Guardians want to stay in business, the boss has to come back—so he will. That is, somebody will. He'll arise, all right."

"Shell," Lyn said, "I know what you mean, of course, and it's not impossible. But you know what Trammel looked like. He was almost a freak."

"He *was* a freak. Maybe they'll get some thin egg and squeeze his head together in a vise, but they'll get somebody and make him up so he looks enough like their boy. The resurrection will probably come off on a dark night and a thin guy with a beak like Trammel's will leap up shouting hallelujahs. The handful of believers present won't get a good look at the fake and he'll be whisked off after five seconds. Word spreads from mouth to mouth, and presto! The Master will have risen. How does it sound, Dr. Nichols?"

"I'd better take your pulse, Mr. Scott. But, seriously, you might be right."

We batted it around a while, then let it lie. The last thing I said about it was "I could be wrong. Let's wait and see."

We didn't have long to wait.

113

Los Angeles was headed for the cackle factory.

The next three days, Friday, Saturday, and Sunday, were the craziest, most fantastic, goofiest that even L.A. had ever seen. It was a slow explosion, a three-day time bomb, and even for those of us smack in the middle of the thing, it was difficult to believe.

Even on Friday, the very next morning after I'd said, "Let's wait and see," I was convinced that the Guardians were going through with a real, right-before-your-eyes resurrection. Friday was the "First Day," time being counted, apparently, not from the exact moment of Trammel's death, but from Thursday, when the rumor had started. And on Friday the whispered rumor had already become, comparatively, a shout.

Even then there was an indication of how big the thing would become. Nobody knew at the moment the peculiar speed with which it would snowball and spread; nobody would know until later, when accounts would come in from widely separated places. But on Friday, even then, the germ of frenzy and fanaticism was present and growing. At first, though it hit the newspapers, it was just another story, a line or column here and there, but by Saturday, the "Second Day," it was big.

It was big enough for the first time to crowd me out of some of the local stories, and it got a surprising amount of space. Primarily it was just an interesting story, something novel to yak about, and naturally not many people of the million or more who read it took it seriously.

But by this Second Day excitement among the Trammelites, among the myraid other cults, even among many of the ordinary everyday citizens of Los Angeles, had grown to fever pitch. The belief, the frantic hope grew, and the rumor had become a slogan mouthed by the faithful: Trammel will arise! Though the fever was fairly well localized among the odd balls, the unstable, the crackpots, it was frightening that so many men could so quickly believe so patent a lie.

Saturday morning the forthcoming resurrection in a sense became official. The Guardians themselves announced to a number of Trammelites that on Sunday at three o'clock in the afternoon Arthur Trammel would be reborn. I even knew the approximate location they mentioned. I'd been in the area half a dozen times for target practice or plinking at tin cans set at the base of a cliff out there;

it was only a few miles from L.A., near a small town named Hollis.

I found it hard to believe, but it had been picked up by the newspapers and was in announcers' words over the air —treated a bit facetiously, usually, but reported nonetheless.

Lyn and I had been talking about it, and I said to her, "All they've got to do is get the resurrection itself accepted. If the followers think Trammel is risen, they'll believe he can do anything—and will the money roll in? I hope to tell you. There'll be Trammelites everywhere you look; those Guardians will be billionaires."

Lyn was frowning. "Shell, Thursday night I went along with you; it was logical enough, and still is. But it doesn't look like this is going to be just a little affair for a handful of Trammelites. And not by the light of the moon, either. They must be pretty sure of themselves."

"Yeah. That's what stumps me, too. I think I can figure the whole works except how they'll find a guy that even with make-up and falsies and what not would look enough like Trammel. Except for that, it's just a large-scale con game. And *if* they pull the caper off tomorrow, the Guardians won't have any trouble explaining why the All-High doesn't go down among the congregation for a while, which he won't. Hell, maybe he's weak; being dead a few days does things to a man. They've got a hundred angles they can use. For one thing, they've got those recordings of Trammel's own voice, his speeches and sermons and get-hot licks."

Lyn said, "It certainly looks like they're going to give it a try."

"They've got to or go out of business. Nobody'll get close to Mr. Fake-Trammel for a while, anyway. After enough time the crowds will acept him as the Trammel they've always had, even if he grows another head. And here's a thought: He could grow a beard. No matter what this Joe Smith actually looks like, he'll just be Trammel with a beard. Hell, there's a thousand tricks they can pull —just so nobody gets a good look at him tomorrow."

"They probably won't, you know."

"True, but I'll bet they'd shout, 'Trammel is risen!' and fall down in faints and fits if John L. Lewis popped out of a hole tomorrow. Except for one thing. I still don't see how the Guardians can find anybody who resembles

Trammel enough, when they've only got three, maybe four days to hunt around. Not in just . . . in— Well, I'll be goddamned."

All of a sudden I knew the answer to every single thing that had been nagging and puzzling me since Trammel had been killed. "What," I said, "are we talking about? Those Guardian eggs didn't have just three days to look for a new Trammel. They had a month, half a year. They had all the time they wanted. Why, hell, *they* murdered the bastard."

Lyn said, "What?"

"You heard me right. I don't know why—maybe the Guardians wanted the gravy, or the glory, or maybe Trammel was just too damned stinking to live—but they knocked their boy off. And they did it when they were ready. So that's how come they're still going ahead with it even now that it's spread all over."

For the first time I felt really satisfied about all the factors surrounding Trammel's death: the apparent coincidence of his being killed while all eyes were on him; the *way* he'd died, in that awful explosion. The only answer was that the others, his murderers, had planned it to look like an accident; they'd wanted thousands to see it happen, wanted all the Trammelites, the more the better, to see that torn, ripped body, know without reservation or doubt that Arthur Trammel was irrevocably, messily dead. Then, when the "new" leader they'd chosen for their new front man, after maybe a year's search or more, arose or climbed from his coffin, and the Trammelites accepted him, then a true miracle would have occurred. I had to hand it to them.

And they damn near had it made, I thought. Actually the only critical part would be the resurrection itself. That was the soft spot—and I'd be right there poking it.

"Something else," I said to Lyn. "Since the Guardians swung into this deal so fast, they must have been ready for a long time, waiting for the psychological moment. And would there ever have been a better moment than Wednesday night? Sunday I'd threatened Trammel, then gone crazy; Sunday night and Monday I was knocking people off like flies, and Monday night I attacked Trammel himself, tried to kill him. At least, that's what everybody believed—what the Guardians wanted them to believe. If Trammel got killed and murder was suspected, the only name that would pop into people's minds would be that of

116

the guy who'd already tried once to kill him: Me. There wasn't any tent meeting Tuesday night—and remember, they wanted the Trammelites to *see* his death—so they took their first chance: the very next night, Wednesday." I thought a minute. "And who did the Guardians accuse? Me, the made-to-order patsy."

We'd got the paper but hadn't yet had time to read it. It was open on Lyn's lap and she looked at it a minute, then said, "The way you talk, you could almost make me believe the Prophet's going to fly this afternoon."

I started to laugh, then said, "The who?"

"Some cultist. The paper says he's going to fly at three o'clock today." She pointed to the item and leaned against my shoulder while we read it together.

There wasn't much, but it was a kick. One "Prophet Lovable," Chief Arbiter for the Lovables of the Sun Kingdom, whatever the hell that was, had announced his imminent departure from earth. Prophet Lovable was going to fly back to the sun. "The sun from whence I came," he was quoted as saying.

The interesting part to me was that Lovable had denounced Arthur Trammel as a fraud, since he, Lovable, was the only man who could come back from the grave. As a matter of fact, he was now in his seventeenth reincarnation. And Lovable stated that he would take off from the very spot at which the impostor would fail to arise.

I said, "Looks like this Lovable cat has gone off the deep end, what with all the excitement. Three o'clock, too— exactly twenty-four hours before the Guardians' operation. The town's cults must be anxious to get in on the act."

Lyn and I were quiet for a while. Finally she slid over onto my lap, put her arms around my neck, and said with her lips close to my ear, "Shell, if the Trammelites believe they've got their leader back, they'll never say anything against him. Not to you or me or anybody. And if the Guardians get away with it tomorrow—"

I interrupted, not even considering what effect my words would have on Lyn. I knew very well how that caper could mess me up, but also what I was going to do about it, and for the moment I forgot I'd meant to keep the idea to myself. I didn't want anybody else to know, because I didn't want anybody else around me when and if I got my arms and legs torn off.

So I blurted it out, just as if I'd already told Lyn about it. "You forget, sweetheart, that no matter how good their facsimile, they'll still have to deck him out with grease paint and doodads to make him reasonable. And you also forget they aren't going to get away with it, since if they try, tomorrow at three o'clock I shall be right there in the thick of things, yanking off falsies or whatever, and raising all kinds of hell."

She didn't quite faint.

She jumped up, shouting things like "You idiot!" and "You suicidal, illogical lunatic!" It went on for a long time. By the time it was over, she knew what I meant to do, had accepted my flat declaration that I *was* going to do it, and had, through her vehemence, her anger, and even her tears, wrung one concession from me. She made me agree that she could go with me clear up to the final moment, with the understood provision that she'd not be near me at the climax.

At two o'clock I said, "Well, since I've got to gander the lay of the land today, we might as well watch the Prophet fly."

"Let's go."

"Who knows, honey? It might be fun. And what are we worried about? Nothing happens till tomorrow, and maybe the whole shebang will peter out before then."

"Maybe," she said. "I'll get my car."

I was on a hill again, with binoculars Lyn had picked up in a pawnshop. This time Lyn was beside me. We were sprawled on the ground far from the spot the Guardians had chosen, and well above it, and through the glasses I could see where tomorrow's resurrection was to be held. The physical props were already in place.

From where Lyn and I lay, the earth sloped downward to a level, bare plain that extended on for another half mile and ended at the base of the cliff where I'd plinked at tin cans. The cliff's smooth face was toward us, jutting up out of the level ground and sometimes rising as much as a hundred feet above it. But from our left and right its upper edge slanted down in a shallow V so that its lowest point was only about thirty feet above the cliff's base on the plain below. That lowest spot, the bottom of the V, had been chosen for tomorrow's resurrection.

Beyond that chosen spot, hills rose even higher and formed a kind of ampitheatre, or bowl, chopped in two at

118

the cliff's edge. From here it looked like the curved half of a huge funnel arcing away from us. The Guardians had picked a perfect place.

The funnel-like bowl was at least twice the size of the L.A. Coliseum, which holds a hundred thousand people, so there would be plenty of room up on those hills beyond the cliff for bug-eyed spectators tomorrow, and they'd all have an unobstructed view.

I swung the glasses left, to the state highway half a mile away, then back. A dirt road ran toward us from the highway, parallel to the cliff and a couple of hundred yards this side of it, then stretched away on our right into the little town of Hollis, which wasn't visible from here. The only other things that marred the level surface of the plain were Hollis' square, concrete reservoir, light glancing from the water in it, and an old abandoned quarry a mile farther to its right.

The coffin wasn't yet in place, and though I couldn't be sure a coffin would be used, it was a reasonable assumption. Near the base of that V on the cliff's edge, a twenty-foot-square area was roped off like a boxing ring and in its exact center was a wooden platform, its top a yard or so above the ground. It was just about the right length and width to hold a coffin.

We were several miles from the Trammelite grounds, but if it seemed odd to me that he wasn't going to arise from the spot where he'd died, it apparently wasn't odd to many other people out here. And that was the first shock—the people.

Through the glasses I could see that already there were more than a thousand men and women gathered over there. Some bedrolls were in evidence, ten or a dozen tents; smoke rose from a wood fire where four women were cooking something.

I handed the glasses to Lyn. "Take a look."

We were alone, all the people being up on the cliff at the center of activity. It was just as well. I still wore my black ensemble, and hadn't made any attempt to disguise my appearance, not only because there was little I could change enough without surgery, but because I'd figured with luck we wouldn't run into anyone. We hadn't. There'd been no real complications to overcome getting here this time; but I still didn't know how I was going to make it tomorrow, clear up to that roped-off area, among thousands of men and women.

119

Lyn said, "I didn't imagine there'd be this many people. You'd think they were giving away something free down there."

"They are. Part of the crowd is undoubtedly composed of Lovables, but I'll bet most of them are just making sure of good seats for tomorrow. What time is it?"

She was on her stomach, and squirmed a bit to look at her watch. "Ten of three." She peered through the glasses again. "That white-gowned chap with the beard must be Lovable."

She handed me the glasses and I found the egg. "He doesn't look very lovable. He doesn't even look likable."

He didn't. I had expected a guy about six feet or so, husky, and with masses of flowing hair. No good reason, just a half-formed idea of what he'd look like, maybe inspired by the positive appearance of his words in the day's paper.

But Lovable, judging by the size of people near him, was barely five feet tall, and pudgy. He was wearing a white robe that reached to the ground and he sported a foot-long gray beard.

"Queer-looking bug," I said. "You know, if he flies, I'm going to feel very creepy about all this."

She laughed, then frowned at me. "Don't talk like that. People don't fly."

"Oh, yeah? You've just been sheltered. People fly all the time." I grinned at her. "You just have to be sure you can do it, that's all. The first inch is the hardest, but after that there's nothing to it."

She made a face at me. "You said you had to . . . what was it? Case the no man's land and plan your getaway route. So case."

I said, "Yep," and used the binoculars some more. Our program was settled—and it was *our* program; there was no longer any argument about it. Lyn would drive me here tomorrow, let me out, then try to park the car somewhere nearby. "So you can run to it," she had told me, "just in case you still have legs on."

"Well, honey," I said, "this is not the most desirable arrangement I have ever seen. As for parking, there would be nothing to it if we were arriving in a helicopter; but there ain't no roads up in them hills. And no place to hide."

She took the glasses again. In a moment she said, "I

120

could hide the car behind the reservoir thing. Nobody could see me from up above it there on the cliff."

"True." It was forty or fifty yards from the spot where all the people were gathered, and right up against the cliff's base. "There is just one small difficulty," I said. "That's a dandy hiding place for you, only I need to be up on *top* of the cliff, so I can pull off noses. I'd better confess, I really don't know how to fly, and—"

"He's flapping his wings!" she shouted. "I mean his arms. He's going to fly—jump!"

"Don't get hysterical!" I shouted.

Lyn slid the left eyepiece to her right eye, leaving room for me to scoot in and stick my left eye before the remaining lens. With a little squirming we got settled so that both of us could see what was going on.

Lovable had earlier been addressing about twenty people, who were in white robes similar to his own, waving his arms about, and wobbling his head like a bell clapper. Right now he was still waving his arms, but he stood on the edge of the cliff, facing us, with his back to the assembled Lovables of the Sun Kingdom.

He made a strange sight, standing there waving his arms up and down. The white-robed people stood in a semicircle behind him. There was some kind of movement among them, but it took me a couple of seconds to discover they were slowly clapping their hands together. I'd have given much to hear them, because they almost surely were chanting some weird thing that would have been interesting.

"He doesn't seem to be going anywhere," Lyn said, and for some reason she was whispering.

I whispered back, "He's not even trying yet. See, they're clapping their hands in time to something. Maybe they're waiting for a sign. Maybe the sun has to split open. Ah, it's in time to his arms."

"I see," she whispered.

It was true. Every time Lovable's arms went up and then came down, all those people clapped. Suddenly they started clapping faster and faster, and Lovable was waving like a fiend up there.

"He's gonna go," Lyn whispered excitedly, "he's gonna go."

There was now a veritable frenzy of motion, of waving and clapping—and all of a sudden all those white-robed

121

people who had been clapping threw their arms up in the air and waggled them. They must have let out a fearful yell at the same moment, because it floated clear up to where we were. It was obviously the end of their chant.

"Here he goes," I said. "Watch him, now. Here he . . ."

Lovable, poor old Lovable, dropped his arms to his sides and looked back over his shoulders. The others slowly stopped waggling their arms.

Lyn said, "Isn't he? Do you think he's going to back out?"

"He can't back out. No more than our friends can tomorrow. He's *got* to fly." I got him in the exact center of my lens and said, "Damn you, *fly!*"

It was as though he heard me. Truly, it was as though he heard me. He swung his head around, eyes front, then raised his eyes heavenward. And then Lovable swept his arms down in a lovely graceful motion and took off for the sun.

He did not, however, get there. He actually went in the opposite direction, down, and broke both his legs.

Chapter Twenty

THAT NIGHT tension started building in me. I was pacing the floor when Lyn grabbed my hand and yanked me down beside her on the couch. Then she crawled up on my lap like a kitten, in that favorite pose of hers—and mine —with her arms around my neck and her lips close to my ear.

"Shell," she said softly, "isn't there another way? Do you have to go out there tomorrow to do it yourself? And all *by* yourself?"

"Yeah, sweetie, and don't talk like an idiot. I shouldn't have to explain why to you. You know what crowds are like, even better than I do. So you know what that one tomorrow will be like."

"I know. Darn it, I know. But how can you do anything alone?"

"I told you, Lyn, no matter if they had ten years to look for the guy they use, if he's to look remotely like Trammel they'll have to gook him up with plenty of make-up, maybe fake eyebrows, a false nose, some porcelain teeth. Well, right about three o'clock I shall pluck off the character's nose, or whatever is handy. And that should get a real rise out of the recently risen Trammel."

"Shell, we haven't talked about this part yet, the part after you unmask him. Assuming you can get close enough actually to do it just the way you hope to. You just told me I know crowd psychology better than you—and I do. A lot better."

"So? Don't give me any speech. *I* make the speeches."

"Shell, listen to me," she said seriously. "Even if it goes perfectly and all of a sudden those people do realize they've been tricked, you can't know their anger won't be directed at you. Not at the fraud, but at the man who *exposed* the fraud. It wouldn't be the first time that's happened. They might turn on you. I know what I'm talking about, Shell."

"Oh, nuts! Why don't you yak about something constructive and shut off this it's-impossible chatter? Why in the name of . . ."

She leaned back a little, but her face was still sober. As my words trailed off she pursed her lips in a kiss.

"I'm sorry, Lyn," I said. "You know I didn't mean anything. I'm wound up like an eight-day clock."

"I know. Get it off your chest."

"It's off. But, hell, you understand I can't do anything else. You know where I wind up if they pull it off. I've got to do it, and right in front of their eyes, too. If I don't, they'll never believe it didn't happen, and you know it. Those characters are experts in rationalization, baby. It has to be right, complete, with no loopholes they can wish their way out of."

"I suppose."

"It's the only way I can prove two things to those believers: that Trammel *is* dead, and that the Guardians are hypocrites and liars. And if I do, everything else the Guardians have done and said will be suspect, including all they've said about me. The fact that they must also have planned this caper long ago will show they must also have planned to knock off Trammel long ago—and one Shell Scott won't look so fiendish any more."

She smiled, and kept smiling. As soon as I grinned, she leaned forward and pursed her lips in a kiss that was not pretended. There was something else I'd been going to tell her, but I'll never know what it was.

This was the Third Day, the day of the resurrection.

In three hours it would happen, and I'd be there, and I still didn't know how I could get halfway to that roped-off ring without being recognized and stopped, much less clear inside it.

Lyn said, "Sit down, Shell. Relax. You'll wear yourself out." I had virtually paced a hole in the carpet. I stopped, slumped on the couch beside Lyn, and said, "Here it is noon again. Big day. I ought to be out there now. But I don't want to get stopped before I even get started on my mission."

"You . . ." She stopped. Since early morning we'd discussed dozens of possible disguises, anything that might get me through, and none of them had been good enough. Lyn probably hesitated at mentioning another feeble one. But she went on: "You might go as a woman. Dress up in—"

"Oh, Lord. Lyn, in the first place, I wouldn't dress up as a woman for any reason. Too damn many comedians and lodge members think that's funny now. Besides, how many six-foot-two and two-hundred-and-five-pound babes have you laid eyes on?"

She shook her head. "Maybe there isn't any way."

"There's always a way."

"Like a way to fly? Shell, I don't want you to go there."

"Uh-uh, baby. We dropped that. That guy just didn't know how to fly, anyway. He went at it wrong. Besides, he didn't have any feathers. Oh, the hell with him." I was jumpy.

"I could stuff cotton in my cheeks, dye my hair—even shave my blasted hair off; I could do a lot of things. But I'd still be a big six-two. Out in the crowd of people, a lot of things might be good enough. But there won't be a hell-uva lot of time; old Whoozit won't be sticking around long. So I've got to be right up there, right in front of a jillion people, and ninety-nine per cent of them will know my size, my shape, and how many hangnails I've got. Oh, Lord, the place is packed already—it was packed yesterday. If I could only shrink!"

It was true enough that almost everybody would know me, and almost certainly be looking for me. Trammel wasn't the only attraction today; this was a double feature. The way the papers were playing up the coming resurrection, you'd think it was the end of the world, but

I hadn't been forgotten. Nearly every reporter and feature writer in California had come up with the same idea. Since the maniac had attacked Arthur Trammel, then murdered him, and finally disappeared "into thin air," it naturally followed that the maniac would be in attendance at the resurrection. That's what they'd said, anyway.

And that was why no disguise had yet sounded good enough. Maybe Lyn was right; maybe there wasn't any. The newspapers and broadcasts had asked the same question about both Trammel and me: Will he return? It was a very disgusting affair as far as I was concerned. The news boys had taken what was a pretty fair story all by itself, tied me into it, and made this the damnedest story that L.A. had ever heard of. It wasn't just local; it was all over the States. For all I knew, it was all over the world. And I wished it were just all over.

Lyn said helpfully, "At least we've got a pretty good getaway planned."

"Yeah. Good enough." I was twitchy, because I knew I was going through with the plan even if I had to strip naked, plaster myself with feathers, and go as a bird. The getaway part, the route and all, Lyn and I had settled yesterday and last night here in her apartment. It would do, but it didn't appear at this point that we'd be using it. I'd found out one other thing last night. Lyn had driven me near the two-story house and the garage where I'd parked my Cad. The car had still been there, with no cops in it, so they must not have found the buggy. From the trunk I'd taken a ten-pound bag of things called tetrahedrons, which bag was now in Lyn's Chrysler convertible, but it didn't appear we'd use them either.

I got up and started pacing again. "I wish I were two feet high," I said. "I wish I could shrink. I wish I were somebody else."

"Shell!" Lyn sounded excited and I swung around toward her. She was getting up off the couch. "Maybe you can shrink. Couldn't you walk on your knees, like José Ferrer in 'Moulin Rouge'? Put pads on your knees and tie your feet up against your thighs?"

The excitement in me started to die down. And then all of a sudden it roared up in me like an explosion and I shouted. "Oh, baby, you're beautiful, wonderful!" I grabbed her about the waist and swung her off the floor and in a circle clear around me.

Then I put her down and said, "No, I can't shrink. But I can do better than that."

"What? Better?"

"Yeah. And how."

I told her. And then there was frantic activity. It took a precious hour, and we had to get in touch with Randolph Hunt again and let him in on it. He not only offered us his lodge as sanctuary if I lived, but spent money and pulled the strings that got us everything we needed. At precisely one-thirty-five I was in the bedroom, all set, and Lyn was alone in the front room waiting for me.

When I walked slowly and awkwardly out of the bedroom she squealed with delight, though she might possibly have gone out of her mind if she hadn't been in on the whole business. Because, aside from Lyn's pancake make-up and eyebrow-pencil pockmarks on my face, I was six feet, eleven inches tall and looked as if I weighed three hundred pounds. I wore a tattered black robe that reached to the floor, had long, long black hair and a long, long black beard that flowed down my chest, and I carried a gnarled staff.

Enter the Prophet! Enter the Master of the Moon People!

Enter Lovable Shell Scott.

Chapter Twenty-One

LYN, instead of suddenly dying when she saw me, let out her happy squeal and said, "Oh! How wonderful you look!"

"Of course." I wiggled bushy, black, glued-on eyebrows at her.

She made a sound suspiciously like gagging, then eyed me up and down. "I think you'll work," she said. "I think if anything would pass, this ghastly whatisit will pass."

"You're right. I don't believe anybody in the world—cops, Trammels, Trammelites, not even Shell Scott—would look for a six-foot-eleven-with-a-black-beard-and-so-on Shell Scott. I am the Purloined Letter. I am cagey as hell. All these cops, all these people, will be looking for a two-foot-high Shell Scott. Aren't I clever?"

"You are nauseous. You are not my love."

"Good. I don't want to be your love, not while I'm in this shape. But just wait till this is over and I'm—"

I saw the sudden pain that marked her face. Her features smoothed almost immediately, but the kicks were gone. I looked at my watch, strapped with its face inside my wrist so I could more unobtrusively check it later. It was time for us to leave.

About a mile from the resurrection spot we got one short glimpse of the crowd, and Lyn gasped, "My God, there must be at least fifty thousand people there!" I told her that plain old garden-variety revivalists often pull ten thousand customers from L.A.'s two million. Fifty thousand for this was almost disappointing. We drove the rest of the way in silence.

She parked at the side of the road; we could see a small segment of the crowd from here.

"Well, off we go," I said, "into the wild bluenoses yonder."

"Oh, stop it," she said. "I know you don't feel funny at all."

"I feel funny as hell, not to mention the way I look."

"Shell, please." Her voice was stretched tight. "It's . . . almost here," she said. "Don't be glib, as if you're off on a lark."

"All right, honey. I was just making words. To tell you the truth, I don't know what I'm saying."

"There you go again. Shell, tell me, how *do* you feel?" Her voice was shaking.

"Well," I said, "I can't say I'm overjoyed. As a matter of fact, I'm scared of that—that bomb up there." I looked out the window, up the rise of ground to the shifting movement and color of the crowd. "But think how bad it would be if it was people."

"Oh-h, *Shell.*" All of a sudden her face was twisted, with tears suddenly starting. She said my name over and over again, grabbed me, wrapped her soft arms around my neck, and clung to me with surprising strength. "Shell," she sobbed, her body shaking against me. "Shell, please, *please* don't go. Forget it, we'll go away somewhere together."

I pulled her arms gently from around my neck. "Lyn, listen to me. I've come all the way up to here, and I'm not going to stop now. I can't."

"Please—"

"Honey! Where would I go? Where would we go? We settled all this. Both of us said we wouldn't talk about it."

She sniffed noisily, pressed both hands over her eyes. Finally she lowered her hands and looked at me, dark streaks of mascara on her cheeks. She took a deep breath and said, "All right. God, you're a mess." She swallowed. "Well, go light your bomb."

I pushed the car door open and swung my legs out, got to my feet, and almost fell. I said. "Hell, honey, it'll be all right." She started the car. I turned around and began walking.

From down on the highway, east of that natural amphitheatre, I had been able to see only a segment at the top of its western arc, and a small part of the crowd. Now, walking on a newly scuffed path in the brown earth, walking slowly and carefully up the slight rise, I could hear the hum and buzz made by thousands of voices a hundred yards ahead of me. On my right was the edge of the cliff slanting sharply ahead, up to its peak, then dropping down, I knew, to the lowest point and the focus of the crowd that would be gathered there. Beyond the cliff, the lower level of the plain stretched toward green hills, and I could see the place where Lyn and I had lain yesterday.

It was difficult and tiring to walk because of the concentration necessary to keep from falling. My added nine inches of height were provided by small lightweight aluminum stilts—until today, appropriately enough, part of a circus clown's bag of tricks. Each was equipped with two leather straps, one tight around my ankle and the other fastened below my knee.

The black robe trailed the ground and hid my feet and stilts, covered my own clothes beneath it. Walking the last few yards, I leaned my weight on the long staff. I could feel the unfamiliar beard warm upon my face, brushing against my chest, and the mass of tangled black hair thick on my cheeks, corded strands dangling over my eyes. Perspiration formed on my face and chest, though the sun was behind one of several low-handing clouds drifting overhead.

I walked the last few steps to the crest of the rise, beyond which the earth sloped down to the place of resurrection. Even knowing what was there, having from a distance seen the people, I wasn't prepared for what I saw now. The ragged outer fringe of the crowd began well below me, extending in a loose circle around to the opposite arc and back to this side again, filling the depression down to the bottom of the earthen funnel. There, two hundred yards away, was the empty square, roped off. People were tightly packed all around it, shoving in closer.

In the square's exact center, already in place upon the wooden platform, was the coffin. When I saw it, saw the harsh angular lines of the coffin in that barren square, so still and somber in contrast to the movement and color all around it, a tingle brushed my spine and prickled my skin.

I swore to myself. I damn well wasn't going to get all creeped up—the way everybody was supposed to—by the clever props, the near perfect location, and all the rest that had obviously been so well and carefully arranged.

When I pulled my eyes from the coffin I saw two blue-uniformed policemen five yards away, and barely managed to keep from breaking into a run. Dozens of other uniformed men were all around the perimeter of the crowd; the place was loaded with cops. Probably more were down in the crowd itself, but these were away from its edge, where they could see anybody who came here.

Both cops were staring at me curiously, their mouths slowly closing, which was just as good as their telling me that I was a very odd sight indeed. So I waved my arms at them and shook my staff at them and said, with my voice as low as I could get it, "Sinners! Oh, you dirty sinners. You have had it." Or something like that, which was about as close as I could get to prophet talk. Then I turned and walked slowly down the hill, leaning on my staff.

I managed ten steps before glancing over my shoulder. One of the men were making circular motions with his index finger near his temple.

As I neared the edge of the crowd I tried to estimate its number. People were scattered in small bunches on the slopes, and only farther down, around the square, were they massed tight. I guessed that fifty thousand wouldn't be any exaggeration. Farther down it didn't look like people at all, but like a vat-dyed ant heap, a blob of squirming animals in all colors of the rainbow. As I walked closer, the sun slid from behind a cloud and

129

in brighter light the colors became more intense, surprisingly varied and vivid.

And now, entering the fringe of the crowd and gathering many, many glances from wide-eyed men and women, I noted something that I had expected here but had not imagined would be present in such wild and staggering profusion: There were more strange forms of life about than I had believed existed.

Not even counting the piles of blankets and bedrolls, the fires and coffee and sandwiches and tents, this was the goddamnedest, goofiest vista of cuckoos I had ever laid eyes on in my life. There were more robes and turbans and crowns and gowns than you could shake a wizard's wand at. There were guys dressed in gold and pink and polka dots, guys in sheets and shrouds and very little; there were dolls in Mother Hubbards, and what appeared to be bras and diapers, and even one babe in grass skirt and beret.

And, of course, it figured. It was sheer inevitability. Not just because this was so close to Hollywood, though that probably helped a lot, but because this was L.A., the Land of the Abnormal. Nobody even tries to deny it any more; L. A. is the magnet for meatballs. It seems that as soon as a citizen from elsewhere loses his stability, he heads for the land where more people are nowhere: Southern California.

We've got, you can count them, over three hundred separate cults. Their membership totals from up in the thousands down to one, and without doubt every member was here. It couldn't have been otherwise. This was the Rising of Trammel, the Big Day.

That meant, too, that over three hundred cult leaders were present—worrying, sweating, biting off fingernails. Their leadership was threatened. If this boy came up today, so would their lunches; they'd lose not only prestige, but their flocks, which would be flocking to Trammel.

So this was an eerie sight indeed. Undoubtedly some here were just curious, and there would surely be reporters and photographers and more cops, but this was primarily a cultists' convention, a crackpot ball. Even for me, after living thirty years in L. A., and knowing that cults and peculiar sects abound from Main Street to the Hollywood hills, seeing all of them in one place at one time was a revelation. It made me think maybe all us people should be in cages, with the animals outside peering in at us, feeding us peanuts and bananas and getting a good laugh.

I went striding downhill through that panorama of paranoia, and *everybody* eyeballed me. Even in this bunch I stood out. Every once in a while some peculiarly decked-out cat, probably a leader surrounded by his followers, would make a strange sign at me or speak as I passed. I ignored them all.

At fifteen minutes of three I had worked my way around to Coffin Square's west side. I could see people in the square, six of them, all dressed in black and lined up facing away from the cliff's edge. And I began wondering seriously how in hell I was going to get up there. Already the going was tough, and there remained a hundred feet between the square and me. It would be anti-climactic indeed if, after all my sweat and preparation, Joe Smith leaped up laughing and waving and I could only wave back at him.

I figured I could press ahead through and around people all right except for the last five or six yards, where bodies were shoulder to shoulder and thigh to thigh and no telling; but from that point on I'd need a dis-integrator. A short fat man facing away from me blocked my path and I was about to step around him when he glanced over his shoulder and saw me. I kept forgetting, momentarily, what I looked like, but he got the full impact of me all at once, and it seemed likely he'd *never* forget.

He must have seen several things today that were pe-culiar, but there was no doubt at all that he had not yet seen anything as horrible as me. You'd have thought his two eyes were attached to his mouth, the way all three of them sprang open. The rapidity of the change and the gruesome fixity of his new expression came close to being the funniest thing I'd seen up here—and all of a sudden I realized that around me were not beings from another world, but just people.

People like me, some of them nearer the edge than others. About the only really tough ones were down in that ring; and if the rest were anything like this joe, I might have it made. With that thought, inspiration blossomed.

From where I stood, the ground slanted downward all the way to the square. So not only was I horrendously tall to begin with; I towered even farther above those ahead of me simply because I was on somewhat higher ground. The guy was still anchored there, gawping up at me as if he were trying to break his neck with his chin.

I swung my staff forward, clutching it back of center, and pointed it at him, mumbling gurgling gibberish deep in my throat. He sprang back from the point of my staff as if it were loaded. I had my disintegrator. I kept walking forward, gargling my tonsils, not too vigorously, but loud enough so those closest could hear me.

With their eyes pointed toward the coffin, naturally none of the people were, at first, looking in my direction. Ah, but afterward they were. One or two before me would hear an odd snuffling noise and turn casually to see a bearded giant, face contorted and eyes glittering, bearing down on them and aiming a wicked gadget at their chops. And then they would not be before me. I did it about twenty times, and I got quite good at it.

And then I was there. It was a tight squeeze, and then a tight fit, but I was against the ropes ten feet from the coffin.

Suddenly my palms were sweating and my throat was dry. I clutched the staff I carried, leaned my weight on it, and breathed heavily through my mouth.

It was five minutes till three. Five minutes until the time of the resurrection.

Chapter Twenty-Two

UNTIL THIS MOMENT I'd been moving, going forward. But now I had time to think. And my thoughts suddenly changed.

What had seemed funny a few minutes ago didn't seem a bit funny now. The moment when I'd first thrust my staff at the fat man and he'd leaped aside had been amusing then; now I thought of what it really meant: that these people all around me were in a mood to believe anything, conditioned to it and ready for it.

I raised my head and looked past the rim of the cliff to my left, at the flat earth and the dirt road slicing through it. Then I turned, looked farther left and behind me, up the slanting ground. I could see the bushy shrub I'd marked in my mind yesterday. It would have been completely hidden by men and women now except that it was at the very edge of the cliff and most of the people stood a few feet away from it.

Lyn would be below there in her car, parked on the far side of the reservoir, the only place where the car could be hidden except for the quarry, a mile farther away. I glanced over the men between there and where I stood, then turned to look inside the square—at the Guardians.

I had become so accustomed to the continual clamor of voices that it was like the withdrawal of a physical pressure when it slowed and got fainter, then suddenly stopped. I knew that men here must have heard the sound momentarily grow fainter and, in a natural enough re-action, themselves stopped speaking. But it was almost as if they had all become silent after an unheard signal. Then the murmur began again.

And suddenly a thought jarred me. I had forgotten one thing, at least one thing. When I moved I would have to move quickly and surely. And I was still wearing the clumsy extensions on my feet.

It was four minutes till three.

Before I took even one step I had to get the stilts off my feet, but there wasn't any way to bend down and un-strap them, take them off and stand up nine inches shorter than before—not with all these men around me. Even if those closest to me failed to notice, the Guardians wouldn't miss it.

All of them stood on my left, facing the coffin and the crowd, the nearest man only four or five feet from me. None of the Guardians stared fixedly at the coffin; they all let their eyes shift over the crowd, sizing us up, noting the rapt expressions. Anger grew in me at the thought that this one thing might stop me—and then I had the answer.

At least, I'd thought of a way that might work. But even though many faiths were here—and thus the lack of many faiths—I hesitated. Because I meant to kneel as though in prayer and under cover of that movement get rid of those stilts, get ready to move.

Three minutes till three.

I raised my arms high slowly, pressed their palms to-gether, and brought my hands down to my chest, bowed my head. Then I knelt, fumbled beneath my robe, trying

133

to keep my movements hidden. I found the leather straps and pulled them free of the buckles; in seconds I had the aluminum stilts off my feet. I let out my breath in a sigh, and it seemed the entire crowd sighed with me; there was movement on my left and right.

It took me a few seconds to understand what was happening; then I got it. Once I had unconsciously led the way, my movement entered all the other minds here as a suggestion, perhaps for some as a command. The man on my right dropped to his knees beside me. He was the first, but then the man beyond him knelt too. In moments there was motion all around me as men and women moved back and to the side, in quietness and without apparent haste, finding room to kneel. The rest followed like sheep.

In less than half a minute every one of them was kneeling. Anyone still on his feet would have been far more obvious than I had been before, and of all those men and women, not one was standing. I looked at every part of the crowd, hoping I'd see at least one man standing alone, but each of the fifty thousand was on his knees.

Two minutes till three.

I looked to my left, over the bowed heads near me and past the cliff's edge, at that plain below. For a moment it seemed a bare, level plain I had seen before in a dream, through the shimmering outlines of a dead woman's face.

And in that moment I saw in a different way the mass of bodies packed around and near me. It was a wall of men, and I had forgotten this part, too, in my plan. I had known that if I should manage to unmask the fake here, the crowd might turn on me. But I'd planned what I would do, thinking that even then, in the moment of shock, I might have a chance to run and get away. But I'd forgotten how tightly packed the bodies around this square would be.

Silence had fallen again. I looked at my watch, saw the second hand moving; I could hear each separate tick as the hand moved steadily closer to the hour.

One minute till three.

It was dimmer suddenly. A new coldness in the air chilled my skin. I couldn't understand. And then, on my knees, I raised my eyes and looked at the sky above me. The sun had gone behind a cloud. That was all; a normal and ordinary thing that had happened many times before

134

this. I'd noticed it now only because it had happened so close to three.

But a ripple, a rising and falling sigh swept over the crowd and then quickly died. The six in black stood immobile now, staring at the coffin's lid. I looked at the coffin. For it was time; it was three o'clock. It was the moment of resurrection.

And the lid of the coffin moved.

An audible sigh went up from the crowd, billowing out of silence. I stared, myself caught in the emotion that stretched almost tangibly through the crowd.

Gnarled fingers, a white bony hand, appeared beneath the coffin's lid. The giant whisper died. The coffin lid moved upward, through its entire arc, fell outward with a creak that was piercingly loud in the silence.

A white hand gripped each of the coffin's wooden walls.

The man pulled himself to a sitting position within the coffin, his face frozen into immobility, white and calm, the appearance of death upon it.

And the crowd stirred. There was a rushing sound, a gasp of breath, a rising wind from which the first faint voices came. Women sobbed and wailed and men cried out as the man inside the coffin moved.

I shook my head, felt my heart pounding in my chest. I had been almost hypnotized by what I'd seen—and I had been ready for it, expected this to happen. I got my feet beneath me, tensed my leg muscles.

The man was thin, his skin white. I had known that even before this suggestible, hopeful crowd, even with all the careful preparation, the likeness would have to be almost perfect if the Guardians hoped for success. While the crowd shrieked and sobbed around me I made myself stare coldly at the man's face.

He climbed from the low coffin and stood upon the ground. And I moved. All around me there was smashing sound, a booming roar of unintelligible words and phrases, of shouts and screams; and women moved, turned, fell to the ground, moaned and shrieked and sobbed.

My legs uncoiled as I slid between the ropes, stood half erect, and leaped toward the man.

He whirled around, shock staining the whiteness of his face, and as I jumped toward him he shrank back. I slammed my foot against the ground and jerked to a stop inches from him, reached for him, clawing for his face —and in that instant all sound stopped.

My hand froze, almost upon his face. I couldn't move. I was stunned, my mind reeling and shock smashing into my brain. For there was no doubt at all, not the slightest question about the man before me.

It was Arthur Trammel!

Chapter Twenty-Three

I COULDN'T THINK. I knew that Arthur Trammel had been dead, that I had seen his torn, bleeding body, his dead body. But I knew that this man was Arthur Trammel.

I stared at him, at his thin skull and close-set eyes, his teeth and chin and hair and lips. And then I pawed at his face, ripped at the long nose and squeezed his flesh, knowing I wouldn't rip false parts of his face away, that he would still be a dead man come to life.

Only seconds had passed, and through it all the crowd had been numbed by silence. I felt Trammel's hands rip at my own face, pull off my false hair and beard, saw the motion and felt his hands; from the corners of my eyes I saw movement about us, a frantic milling as men and women cringed in fright and horror, some turning away.

Then Arthur Trammel stepped back, raised his left hand, and pointed a long gnarled finger at me. In a voice like the crack of doom, loud and booming in the silence, he cried, "There stands the man who murdered me!"

As his words died away there was a low mutter from five thousand, ten, then fifty thousand throats. It was muted at first, for a long second a nearly constant rumble —and then with a sudden, incredible violence the crowd exploded. It was a scream, a throat-ripping cry of fright and hate, like nothing I'd ever heard before.

From the moment when Trammel had pointed at me and spoken till this moment with sound crashing against my ears, no one had made a move toward me. The movement, when it came, wasn't from the crowd, but from within this square. One of the Guardians, a square chunky man, leaped toward me. His hand clutched at my robe and spun me around—and snapped me out of my own shock.

The square and chunky Guardian had spun me around, but long before I'd turned halfway my left arm was swinging from across my middle, hand stretched open. The hard thick edge of my palm thudded into his mouth and I felt his teeth snap beneath his mashed lips.

All around me was a blur of color and movement; no others were yet inside the square, but I knew they'd soon be rushing in. I figured I was dead already, anyway, and what the hell, I'd bat these beggars with my dismembered limbs as long as I could. So I did the one thing that might shock all these bloodthirsty screechers, if they were still capable of shock. One jump took me to him, to the risen Arthur Trammel, and I hit him on the point of the chin as hard as I could, and he was once more unrisen.

I bent over and grabbed him, yanked his limp body over my head, then turned around and charged across the ring, gathering speed and whooping horribly.

These last ten seconds had affected different people in different ways, and many who had been pressed close about the ring had already drawn back or run from the bolts of lightning or sheets of flame that inevitably would be crackling about me, but there was still an appalling number of people straight ahead of me. I had no time to crawl under ropes, so I just sprinted harder and slammed through them, posts going down and ropes flapping, but I went through. And I threw Arthur Trammel as hard as I could at a flock of about fifty ready-to-faint people.

Some of them fainted. Others got the hell out of the way, either afraid of Trammel or afraid of me. And, too, a lot of them already knew I was a maniac, and that helped. There weren't many who cared to tangle with such as I.

All of a sudden I noticed that, though I hadn't consciously chosen a destination, I had already come uphill about halfway to the funny-shaped bush I'd chosen yesterday. There were still plenty of people between it and me, though most of them weren't looking at me, but behind me at Trammel and the crowd now baying at my heels. I aimed at the bush.

Oh, man, I had done some other running in days gone by, but this was by far the best running I'd done. This time I had *incentive*. I noticed with a kind of detached interest a guy rolling about and a woman throwing dirt in her face, and I guess there were fits all over. That made the going easier for me, but it wasn't all gravy.

Two guys who loomed before me, either petrified or being brave, turned out to be foolhardy and received a fist in their chops. I gave one other guy a shoulder and, terrible as it may sound, straight-armed a woman. But she was a great big broad-shouldered *man* of a woman—and she was, after all, in *my* way.

Only at the very last did I actually start thinking I might make it. Of course, making it wasn't such a hell of a great thing, anyway. You can't be exactly light-hearted about jumping off a sixty-foot cliff.

So I veered away from the cliff's edge in order to get a better crack at that bush. Some people scattered and I dodged whooping around others, and then, when I was almost opposite the bush, I spun right and sprinted toward it.

As I ran toward the edge of the cliff I wondered if I were truly acting in a rational fashion, if this were really what I had so carefully planned. After all that had happened, there was at least a small chance that I was out of my mind. The thought bothered me, but I kept running.

Then I reached the edge of the cliff, leaped from it, flapped my arms, and took off for the sun.

Chapter Twenty-Four

I FLEW NO BETTER than Lovable, for whom the sun had been his undoing, and I went in the same direction he had gone, down. Ah, but I had planned it this way, I told myself. Because, though I was afraid to look just yet, I knew that somewhere down there, right below that bush, was an open reservoir, with several feet of water in it, which reservoir Lyn and I had carefully cased yesterday afternoon. So all I had to do was keep falling, which was no trick at all, and I would, if my calculations were correct . . . Right then a sickening thought struck me:

My God, was that the right bush?

Suddenly I didn't want to go through with it. That was

138

tough. All these thoughts were going through my mind with lightning speed, of course, because all this time I was still falling. Finally I looked down, just in time to see water, and also just in time to realize that I must have been yelling, because as I plummeted into the water much of it filled my open mouth. When I hit the reservoir bottom, the impact knocked the air out of my lungs, but I was conscious, and shoving upward with my legs and paddling.

When my head broke the surface I could hear the roar of the convertible's engine and knew that Lyn must have seen me coming. I hauled myself over the wall and dropped to the ground, ran around to the reservoir's far side, and leaped into the convertible without opening the door. Lyn was gunning the motor in low before I landed.

She didn't say anything, just slammed the accelerator down and started on the route we'd planned. Her face was white and scared, her lips pressed tightly together. At the dirt road two hundred yards out from the cliff she swung right toward the state highway. We'd driven the other way yesterday, and that way the road ended at Hollis.

Lyn glanced quickly at me and spoke. "What happened? I heard the most awful sounds."

"*You* heard some awful sounds. What do you think I—"

The shrill wail of a siren cut through my answer. On our right, coming like a bat out of hell down the state highway toward us, was a police radio car.

"Go," I said. "Go, baby, go."

A second police car was a hundred yards behind the first one; a third followed it. "Oh, murder," I said. "There'll be a thousand cop cars after us in a minute. There'll—"

I stopped because we were almost at the intersection. We were going to make it ahead of that first police car. But we had to turn, and the way Lyn was driving, I figured we'd turn over instead of left.

"Hit the brakes!" I yelled, but she was already hitting them. We slid, skidded sideways, and swerved on the dirt road as she let up on the brake pedal and jammed it down again, yanking the steering wheel left. When we hit asphalt the car shuddered and tires shrieked. I could smell hot rubber and brake lining, then I felt the car tip.

I thought we were going over for sure, and as I started to reach for the wheel she snapped it right, whipped it

139

left again as the wheels banged down on the asphalt. We slid clear over the edge of the road, hit the dirt, then veered back onto the highway. A shot cracked out and I glanced over my shoulder to see the radio car behind, so close I could see the bore of a gun held in an officer's hand. His right arm was stuck out the window by him and it looked as if the gun were aimed squarely at my left eye.

I snapped around, shoved my hands down between my legs to the sack of tetrahedrons ready for me on the floor boards, metal gadgets like a kid's jacks, only multi-pointed and sharp. In the war they were scattered on roads to stop enemy vehicles. This was war, and right now that guy shooting at me was an enemy.

Another shot cracked out and the slug crashed through the windshield as I swung my arms up, clutching a double handful of tetrahedrons, and threw them over my head and behind the car. I reached down for more, tossed them out onto the road, then jerked my head around for a look.

The officer was just about to fire again and kill me when the car's front tires hit a whole mess of tetrahedrons; and then the back ones hit more. There was one bang from the gun, then four almost simultaneous bangs as all four tires blew out. The car jerked, skidded off the road. For a moment I thought it was going over, but the car stayed upright.

Far down the road behind us there was a mass of cars, part of the rabid fifty thousand joining the chase. I got busy, tossed out tetrahedrons until the sack was empty. By the time I finished, the other two police cars were out of commission, one clear off the road and the other partly on it, turned sideways, and the mass of a hundred or so other buggies was almost upon the beginning of the tetrahedron highway. I couldn't bear to look.

I turned around, stared ahead, trying to think.

Suddenly Lyn cut into my thoughts. "What's the matter? You're white as a sheet. And why do you keep saying that?"

"Saying what? I didn't know I was saying anything."

"You keep saying, 'Trammel is risen, Trammel is risen.'"

I wiped sweat off my forehead. "Baby," I said, "believe it or not, he is."

"Oh, my goodness," she said. "Shell, pull yourself together."

"Ha. That's what *he* did. He's back there. I wouldn't be surprised if he's back there in that reservoir dancing around on the water."

"It couldn't have been Trammel."

"Damnit, it *was!*"

"Then he couldn't have been dead."

"He was dead. And now he's alive. I'm nuts, that's all. I'm through. Baby, I'm going to hell. And you know what? I really believe it. I'm going to roast for nine million centuries. Oh, the things I've done! I thought they were worth it, but nine million centuries—"

"Will you stop babbling?"

"Lyn," I said hoarsely, "you haven't been where I've been. You didn't see him. Man, his eyes were like neon tubes, his voice was like thunder."

She took one hand from the wheel and slapped me so hard that little dots danced in front of my eyes. For about five seconds no more was said. Then I grinned at her. "O.K., baby, I'll explain later."

The next twenty minutes were frantic. Twice I stole cars, crossed the ignition wires while Lyn drove on ahead, then drove my stolen buggy after her and picked her up. Two police cars with sirens screaming passed us while we were in a Ford; three while we were in a Chevy. I turned the Chevy's radio on and tried to explain to Lyn what had happened. A news broadcast was on the air.

The announcer paused. "Here is a bulletin just handed me," he said. "Ah—" He stopped, then went on. "Arthur Trammel, dead three days, this afternoon arose from the grave. . . . Pardon me." There was a short silence. "One moment, please." He coughed. "This is . . . ah, the first report and without corroboration. Arthur Trammel, founder of Trammelism and leader of the Guardians, and, ah, dead three days, this afternoon arose from the grave in the presence of a crowd estimated at one hundred thousand persons. He was assaulted by a prophet, alleged to have murdered him, a man whom—who it is reported may have been Sheldon Scott." There was a long pause. "Who it is alleged flew? Flew through the air in approximately the same spot where one Prophet Lovable unsuccessfully flew yesterday."

There was a little more, and the announcer got through

141

it, including the fact that I had escaped in a Chrysler driven by a woman. The license number was given. By now the police undoubtedly had found Lyn's car.

I skidded to a stop at the edge of the road. "Far enough," I said. "Now we walk."

It took six hours of the day and maybe a year off our lives, but just before ten P.M., with the remembered sound of sirens still in our ears, we could see the lights of Randolph Hunt's lodge fifty yards away. I went to it alone, checked with Hunt, and then brought in Lyn.

The following Tuesday, at twelve-thirty in the afternoon, Randy, Lyn, and I sat before logs burning in the fireplace. Jo and Olive, under the circumstances, hadn't been invited. The three of us had read the newspapers, listened to the radio, and watched TV, and Randy had picked up word-of-mouth conversation and whispers that he'd passed on to us.

There had been frenzy in the news before, but now insanity was the order of the day. The word was spreading like hoof-and-mouth disease: Trammel had risen. There were skeptics and disbelievers and men convulsed with laughter everywhere you looked, and the All-High, Trammel himself, had been questioned—ever so politely—by police and other citizens. But nobody could prove he hadn't risen. And everybody was talking about it.

Among the shattered ones, the cults and crackpots, there were rapture and shouting complete with convulsions. All the cults and strange sects were vying with each other, each trying to outflip the next, and it was pathetic the way men hoped for more miracles. All kinds of silly things happened. It was a contagious madness, a galloping dementia, like chain letters or knock-knock; the thing caught on and swept over California like a plague, then headed east.

In Southern California a man calling himself the Great Wun walked into the Pacific Ocean after speaking to his followers and declaring he was going to convert the fish; he floated ashore several hours later, not speaking to anybody. One Yogajondo, Father of the Common People, headed a march of three hundred Common People on Washington, their avowed goal being a guaranteed minimum luxury, including Cadillacs. One King Ramaud jumped from the spot where Lovable and I had flown, landed on his head, and splashed his brains out; it didn't make much of a splash in the newspapers. As for Prophet

142

Lovable, Chief Arbiter for the Lovables of the Sun Kingdom, it was authoritatively reported that he had actually
flown. His white-robed followers had seen him soar into
space. Soon he would return from the sun, bringing light
and gladness.

A thousand other things happened, some crazy, some
silly, all frightening, but they were as nothing compared
to the furor over Trammel—and over me. Here at the
lodge, we'd covered almost everything and come up with
nothing that was any help to me.

"I can't shrink or grow taller, either," I said to Lyn.
"From now on they'll be looking for a guy between one
foot and ten feet tall, with black, red, white, or green hair."

"There must be something . . ."

"Yeah, sure. That Trammel is a damned smart tricky
dog. I went out there to unmask him and he unmasked
me. Now that I look back, I remember when he pointed
at me I saw a watch on his wrist. Didn't mean anything
to me then, but that explains how he timed his move so
nicely. And he was still lying when he climbed out of that
coffin. He said that I was the man who'd murdered him.
Hell, I was maybe the one man in the world who really
wanted him alive."

"Well, he is now," Lyn said.

"That's the one sure thing, that Trammel is now alive
and kicking. Kicking about damn near everything, if I
know him."

Randy said, "Hell, son, ain't it better than if he was
dead?"

"Yeah—if I knew what to do about it. But I'll never
convince his flock that he wasn't resurrected, and as long
as they believe that, they won't believe *anything* against
him. They won't say anything against him, either. I know
enough about him right now to ruin him if I could tell
it, get it believed. Ordering Felicity's death is plenty, but
his murdering Dixon would get him the gas chamber all
by itself."

Randy said, "I never did get the straight of how you
knowed he killed Dixie."

"Simple enough, Randy. I saw Dixon about midnight,
minutes before I killed Wolfe. Within an hour or so after
that I found her body. Obviously someone besides Wolfe
had killed her and buried her. For it to have happened so
fast it almost had to mean she'd got in touch with somebody, who then killed her; or somebody got in touch with

143

her. Makes no difference. The fact that Dixon was in the same grave where Wolfe had just buried Felicity meant that whoever killed Dixon knew what Wolfe had done. He couldn't have just happened to stumble onto that same grave."

I got up and started pacing the floor. "Hell, we know now that it was Trammel. Wolfe and Dixon were the two people taking care of Trammel's pregnant Trammelites, and with Wolfe dead, Dixon was the only one of them left alive to spill what he'd been doing. If that came out, he'd be ruined, down goes the empire, everybody sneers at Trammel. So he bashes her head in and he's in the clear—until wham, he learns I'd found Felicity's body. Naturally he knew I'd found Dixon's first. I knew all about him then—and he knew I did by that time. Damnit, there's enough to hang him, but I haven't any proof really. If I could just get him to spill, get my hands on him and work him over—but you can imagine what would happen to me. And who'd accept my word against the risen Trammel's?"

Lyn was frowning. "Shell, there are about three hundred of those other cult leaders in town, dying for any good reason to discredit Trammel. They're on your side."

"True enough. They hate Trammel more than they hate me, at least," I said slowly. "Damn near every cultist in the area has switched over to Trammel, and those sad three hundred are really sad. If I could only think of something good enough, if I knew *how* he pulled off his miracle . . . But I'm stumped. I have been practically all . . ."

An idea exploded like white rockets inside my brain and I said softly, "I'll be damned. How could I have missed it? And me an ex-Marine. I'll be damned." I looked from Randy to Lyn and grinned. "Wouldn't this kill you?" I said. "I know how he did it."

Chapter Twenty-Five

IT WAS NEARLY nine o'clock Wednesday night and I lay flat on my stomach between the Truth Room and the Trammelite tent, on the spot where Arthur Trammel had

144

died. He was on stage now and I couldn't see him, but I could hear him raving.

Raving to a helluva crowd, too. There must have been close to ten thousand old and new customers present. At the rear and on both sides of the tent the canvas was raised and people overflowed onto the grounds. None of them had spotted me yet, but when the meeting ended and the lights came up for Trammel's customary walk to the Truth Room I would be plainly visible. Especially since I'd be inside the tent.

There were no half-dozen guards around tonight, as there'd been when Trammel had been caught in his explosion. I realized now that guards had been present primarily to assure the success of Trammel's "death," make sure nobody wandered into the danger area before Trammel did. The one man who'd been out here earlier when I'd run in from the shadows was now lying unconscious fifty yards away with a large lump on his skull.

When I'd had my brain-blow yesterday I'd spent another hour figuring out the rest of it. Trammel would have needed help of a certain kind, and though there was no way of knowing who had helped him and the Guardians, I'd known where I could get the same kind of help for myself. I'd gone to an old friend, Irving Feldspen, head wheel of Magna Studios in Hollywood. He'd got in touch with a guy who could fix me up with what I needed, had him come to Feldspen's home. After ten minutes of explanation I'd been able to put away my gun. The guy's name was Bill Grange, he was Feldspen's top special-effects man, and when we'd understood each other I'd told him exactly what I wanted. He'd thought he could handle it. He did.

Everything was ready. Grange had helped me, in this last half hour while Trammel spoke, but he was gone now. There was nobody here but me and Trammelites, all of whom, thanks to Trammel, knew exactly what I looked like. He had shown them photographs of me, just in case one or two didn't already know about me. At the moment he was talking about me, inciting his flock to murder, literally, bringing their hate for me to fever pitch—and he had been doing that ever since he came back. They wouldn't have any trouble recognizing me. My hair wasn't dyed, but short-cropped and white as usual. I wore a brown sports jacket, and ripped copper-colored slacks; under the coat was part of a white shirt and an explosive red-and-yellow tie. In a way, I had my boots on.

145

It was time to start, I got my feet under me and walked forward, carefully lifting my leg over the thin wire Grange had strung there; I couldn't afford to have this deal literally blow up in my face, not yet. I got almost to the tent before the lights came up and anybody saw me. All eyes were on Trammel, but then one woman inside the tent turned her head and stared at me. As she poked a man on her left, Trammel started to walk across the platform—and I sprinted forward into the tent, stopped in front of the crowd.

There was a moment of shocked silence as hundreds of heads turned toward me. They knew immediately who I was. As sound began to rise from the crowd, as I turned to look at Trammel, he saw me. He didn't hesitate, didn't wait. With the mike on his chest amplifying his words, he shouted. "Kill him!"

The crowd surged toward me, yelling, shrieking. I whirled and ran toward the Truth Room, taking the same path Trammel had taken that night when he had died.

Right where Trammel had done it, right where he had died, I kicked the wire Grange had strung there—and for the second time here the night erupted in sound and color as an explosion boomed around me, as smoke swirled and flashlight powder went off in a blinding flare. There was a crash of sound, a whirlwind of smoke and light and fire. I wasn't hurt, but hot winds spun around me, licked at my skin; and though my eyes had been squeezed tight, even my sight was dimmed when I opened them—and looked at carnage.

Those behind me, blinded by that giant flare, wouldn't yet be able to see anything. Smoke and dust billowed as I leaped forward, ripping off my coat and throwing it from me in the same way that Trammel must have ripped off his black outer robe one week ago. Everything was ready and in place. My left leg was ten yards away, near my left arm, and my right leg from the knee down was at my feet, artistically placed. They were disgustingly realistic limbs, though they were only *moulages*, and would be eminently satisfactory as long as nobody picked them up. But people just don't pick up dismembered arms and legs.

The *moulage* angle was what had amazed me yesterday: that I, an ex-Marine who had seen hundreds of such gory-looking, bloodstained rubber imitations of mayhem, shouldn't have realized before how Trammel had pulled himself together. I'd seen many plaster *moulages* used for

146

preserving evidence of a crime, but the Marine items had been almost identical with the real thing—what men would see after a mortar fell or a bomb burst among soldiers on a battlefield. And my legs and arm were works of art, on which Bill Grange had lovingly labored.

At the spot where I'd earlier dug three carefully spaced holes, I flopped to the ground. With my coat off, my chest was bare under my already shredded shirt, except for another particularly gruesome *moulage* of thin rubber, appropriately twisted and red-painted on one side, and as I turned and slid my left leg into one of the holes I ripped my thread-tacked trousers, exposing more gory horror beneath the cloth. In moments both legs were thrust deep into the holes, left leg clear up to my thigh and right leg to the knee; then I added the finishing touches, the two unkindest cuts of all.

On the ground a foot from me, alongside a gallon bag of chicken blood, lay the final *moulage,* the ultimate artistry of Bill Grange. I slipped it over my head, adjusted it rapidly with my hands, being especially careful of the eye. The thin rubber went on easily, a red-and-black puckered patch fitting beneath my left brow, and dangling on thin rubber stalks from that puckered spot hung an eye. I could feel the cold round ball bouncing on my cheek as I picked up the bag of blood.

I had estimated that I'd have about five seconds before the crowd recovered its sense and sight. I counted two as I thrust my legs into their holes, three as I put on the facial *moulage,* four as I burst the bag of blood and splashed it over my face and hair and chest, and on the "stumps" of my legs and left arm. At five I hurled the bag from me and lay back, thrusting my left arm up to the elbow into the third hole. I lay quietly, holding my breath and staring upward at the swirling dust and smoke above me. Then, the most horribly dead dead man that these people would ever see, I waited.

Several more seconds passed before the crowd began gathering around me. Through my right eye I watched horror and disgust and sickness grow on their faces, and all the time I was aware that Trammel knew what was happening. He continued to shout at those still in the tent, but as soon as he'd heard the explosion, immediately after seeing me, he would have known what I was trying to do. He was screaming to the crowd that they must kill me.

And here I was already dead.

Very bloodily dead, at that. I must have been the bloodiest thing in the world. Arms and legs all over. And I was still bleeding pretty well, just as well as Trammel had. Voices stopped and all were solemn in the presence of death.

But in the faces of a few around me there was, with the sickness, a kind of puzzled expression. It would seem strange to some of those who had watched Trammel die that this same odd sequence of events should be happening again. The only difference this time was that nobody was handy to toss a blanket over my corpse, as somebody had for Trammel—at least, that was the only difference you could notice so far.

Even though I knew I might get my real limbs yanked off in the next minute, I was beginning to enjoy this drawn-out moment of anticipation at what I was going to do to these idiots who, a few seconds before, had been ready to drink my blood.

I might even have let my death sink deeper into their brains if I hadn't been afraid Trammel would come tripping out here and shoot the corpse. So I decided to give it a try.

Softly, very softly, barely moving my mashed and bleeding lips, I said, "Hello, you cats."

In the silence around me the words were quite audible. "Hello," I said. "No, not up there. Down here."

Several people got even more sick looking. Nobody could figure out where that sepulchral voice was coming from. I pushed it a little farther.

"This is me. You think I'm dead, don't you? Well, I'm not. Ha-ha, I'm fooling you."

No one could understand this. One woman was gawking at me, squarely at me, and she was a perfect picture of one who is not believing what she is seeing. I stared right back at her from my one good eye, and for all I knew, the other eye was staring at her from my cheek, and on an impulse I twitched my lips and winked at her.

She let out a short "Ack-k-k!" and her eyes rolled up as she fell kerplop on the ground.

I said, more loudly, so that none of those around me would miss it—and there must have been at least a thousand massed behind those closest to me—"Nope, I'm just about to spring up at you. Man, I bet you scatter. I'm gonna arise, kids! This is the Shell Scott resurrection!"

And with that, while faces blanched and became puttylike, I yanked my legs and arm from the ground and sat up straight, surrounded by the goddamnedest collection of expressions imaginable. Then I jumped up and yelled at them.

"Now, you bloody believers," I shouted, "now you know how Trammel did it!"

Chapter Twenty-Six

AT LEAST THREE or four more people fainted, including one frail man close to me, and then there was the wildest shrieking and wailing and gnashing of teeth imaginable.

People fell down and whooped and hollered; people ran screaming to the revival tent—and that was part of what I wanted. When I went in after them, I wanted some there ahead of me who had seen me die, and some who had seen me die and then arise. Everybody got away from me fast, and there was almost as much dirt stirred up by stampeding feet as there had been by the explosion.

I gathered up all my arms and legs and ran like a fiend to the tent, some of the crowd following me, some fleeing screaming ahead of me, and then I ran up onto the stage, where Trammel was shouting, his voice amplified by the chest mike until it sounded like Joshua's trumpet at Jericho.

I stepped two yards from him, turned to the milling crowd, and yelled at them. I couldn't touch the Master yet, because, limbs or no limbs, his followers would fix me. But for once nobody was looking at Trammel; all ten thousand or so were eyeballing me.

And, I suppose, with reason. Every one of those people out there knew I must be alive, but they must also have wondered how I could be. I showed them.

There was so much noise that I could hardly hear Trammel myself, and I started with my eye, the dangling one. I yanked it from its stalks and threw it out into the crowd like a posy. People jerked and screamed and leaped away, and naturally more people fell down. Some of them got trampled on, but I didn't mind. In fact, I liked it; I'd have been glad to trample on some of them myself. Because a minute ago they'd been chasing me to kill me, to murder the hell out of me, and maybe in another minute they'd get me. But for right now it was my happy moment, and I was getting the most out of it.

I gave them an arm, then a leg, and I saved the long bloody leg and thigh till last. There was gasping and wailing, but I let out a whoop as I grabbed my ankle and with all my strength threw my left leg high into the air. It went away up toward the canvas ceiling, turning almost majestically, then it came down toward a pile of screaming people and landed on the floor, because though the people were still screaming, they had moved.

For just a few seconds I had a chance to make myself heard. As I ripped the *moulages* from my chest and head, a near silence fell. Not even Trammel was speaking.

"You saw me die!" I shouted, and they heard me. "The same way you saw Arthur Trammel die. And his death was a trick, just as mine was a trick. Take a look, you goddamned bloodthirsty beggars. Those are rubber!"

I didn't have time to get it all out. Trammel was always in there pitching, always battling, even when his back was against the wall. With that voice they had heard for so long, the lilting voice they had believed and even loved, Arthur Trammel began working upon their minds and emotions, still plunging ahead with his unswerving con, trying to gather his flock around him and knit their dream together. He talked and sighed and ranted and raved, started to weave the familiar spell over them, and the people, because they wanted so desperately to believe in him, began believing.

He was close to making them believe that this actually hadn't happened, that I didn't exist, was a hallucination. But I hadn't come here completely unprepared for this moment. From the stage I could see a number of queer faces, some of them faces I'd seen before. Part of the planning for this had been an attempt to reach and assure the presence here tonight of all the three hundred-odd leaders of other odd cults in L.A.—the men who had plenty of reason to hate and denounce Trammel. I could see some of them there below me, and I knew most of the three hundred must have responded to my invitation.

Some were coming close now, pushing toward the stage. Trammel had the edge, sure, and maybe my voice wouldn't reach to the back of the tent, but I could sure as hell make those closest hear me. And they were hearing. Because I wasn't just standing there listening to Trammel; I was

150

yelling like a foghorn, ripping my throat, getting hoarse, but laying it all out there: Trammel's lies and sex and murder and fraud, Felicity's death and Dixon's, the tape-recorded tricks, all of it that I could get in.

There were just the two voices, Trammel's and mine. The others were listening to us, not screaming or shouting any longer. All were standing, and there wasn't any empty space at the edge of the stage; men and women were massed there, eyes raised to stare at the two of us.

The Leader appeared frightened. And I'd been trying to frighten him. When I'd realized I could reach those men and women nearest me, I'd realized I could also reach Trammel, make him hear me. Many of the words I'd shouted had been for Trammel, to let him hear how much I knew. He'd heard me, and he was frightened.

Those in the crowd hadn't yet grasped either idea completely: that I had profaned their idol, or that their idol had tricked them, lied to them, and deceived them. But they were restless. There was movement in the crowd and suppressed violence in that movement.

Trammel's voice had faltered, but in a moment when I paused for breath he seemed to gather strength and power of mind again. He pointed at me and with his voice strong said, "You know he is mad."

That was all, but it reminded everyone here of the things they'd heard and believed of me in these last days. And all of them turned to look at me. They had followed Trammel too long, and I knew that unless Trammel himself broke, I was finished. There was movement below me as a man, one of my three hundred, stooped and picked something from the ground. I could see his fist close around it as he rose. I walked closer to Trammel, stood almost against him, and I started talking fast, directing every word at him.

"Figure it out, you sonofabitch. You're through. No matter what this bunch does to me, you're finished. Maybe not now, not even today, but tomorrow or the next day, when they aren't listening to your voice, they'll figure it out. Enough of them will."

While realization was growing in his mind, I finished it. "No matter what happens this minute, Trammel, you've got to run. Enough of them below us heard the things I said. They know about your slimy tricks and lies—enough of them do."

His face seemed to crumple, to sag. I saw the movement

151

near us in the crowd, but I watched Trammel, and got ready to pull or shove him into the path of the missile if one came, but I didn't have to. The man below us drew back his arm and hurled a clot of earth that struck Trammel on the chest. He looked down at the mark it left on his black robe, his face ashen.

He turned his head and suddenly leaped for me, hands clutching at my face, but as he reached for me I stepped aside, shoved him, and he fell. He sprawled on the platform, almost going over its edge, as a whispering sound swelled from the crowd again. Hands reached for him. In that moment Trammel must have thought they meant not to help him, but to hurt him. He shrank back, crying out softly, got to his feet, and half ran toward the steps leading from the stage.

For a moment he paused there as sound swelled to an angry roar; and even then I didn't know if it was meant for him or me. But Trammel was unnerved and shaken, frightened, and he ran.

He ran from the tent, raced toward his Truth Room, and the crowd was still, shocked and nearly silent. For he was so obviously frightened and abject, so obviously not godlike. Either those in the crowd suddenly knew what he was or they acted without knowing, without needing to know. They ran after him. It was one man at first, but the rest of the mass surged forward then, became part of the initial movement. They were shouting, screaming. They were going to kill him.

I ran from the stage and was caught in the mass of men and women. I fought to get free, then burst from the crowd's edge, but I didn't know where Trammel was, or even if he were alive. Then I saw men pouring into the low-roofed Truth Room, and I sprinted to it but couldn't get through the bodies that jammed its door—and inside the room there was the most awful sound, the cry of voices roaring steadily, a thousand men shouting and cursing.

I reached the wall, followed it to the building's rear, and ran through the cloth-draped entrance into bedlam. I fought my way to the raised wooden podium, and from there I could see a swirl of movement in the room's center, where I knew Trammel must be. It would have been impossible to force my way through that mass of men to the one man I wanted to keep alive—but in front of me was the microphone Trammel had used here on so many nights, beneath it his recorder ready for the taped speech he had meant to deliver at this hour. I switched the microphone on, put my mouth close to it, and shouted as loudly as I could. But even my amplified voice was lost in the clamor and the words had no effect.

For seconds longer the milling and shouting continued in the crowd's center, then it slackened. Gradually emotions died, pulses beat more slowly. Finally all motion stopped and there was silence. And in that silence there was the high wailing of a woman's scream.

That scream started a ripple of movement, an edging away from what little was left of Trammel. The ripple spread, and from the raised platform I could see men draw back from a crumpled figure in the room's center. The movement spread like panic; it gathered momentum as quickly as mindless lust had gathered in the beginning. Men poured from the door and into the night, crushing against each other in their anxiety to get away.

Soon they all were gone. Only Trammel's still body and I were left. He looked small, twisted, and ugly, less a man than a bundle of bloodstained rags.

And then Trammel moaned.

I stared at him, not comprehending, because I had been so sure they must have killed him. But he moaned again, and moved.

I started to run toward him, then saw again before me, bolted to the podium's wooden frame, the recorder on which a spool of tape had earlier been wound in readiness for Trammel's Truth Room fraud tonight. I turned back to it, twisted the recorder's switch from "Play" to "Record" and the volume high, then turned the machine on. The small hand mike was free but its wire stretched barely to the floor, still twenty feet from Trammel. I ran to him, picked him up in my arms as he gagged and a small line of blood spilled from his mouth. I carried him carefully, but not because I wanted him to live; I wanted him to talk a while before he died.

I eased him to the floor, held the microphone to his mashed lips as he moved again.

He moaned, a sigh that was barely audible. "Trammel," I said, "You're dying. Can you talk?"

The redness of his mouth moved but for long seconds no sound came from it. Then, "Yes," he said. "Yes. I mustn't die. Don't let me die." The words were twisted, but understandable.

153

"Then talk fast, mister. Tell me the whole thing. About Felicity, the other little Trammelites you played with, Wolfe and Dixon and the hell you gave me, the lies, all of it." I looked at his mashed face and torn body, white bone protruding from one broken arm, and I knew that he'd soon be dead.

"Help me," he moaned. "Don't let me die."

"I can't help you, Trammel."

"I . . . can't . . . can't be dying."

"You haven't got much time."

He coughed, and he must have felt the new rush of blood from his mouth. For seconds he was silent, then he said weakly, "Will you help me? If I tell you . . . will you help me? Please . . ."

"I won't promise you a damn thing, Trammel. Except that if you don't spill fast, I'll help you die. Maybe only a minute sooner than you would anyway, but sooner."

Finally he accepted it, thinking I could help him if he told me everything, and maybe even believing that if I could help him I would. I held the microphone before his mouth. His voice whispered into it, and over the words he had recorded days or weeks before on the now unwinding tape, erasing those words as he spoke, was impressed most of what I'd wanted him to tell.

And most of it was the way I'd figured it, the way I'd told Lyn it had to be, his phoning Wolfe right after I left him that Sunday, telling him to kill Felicity, who had just been aborted of Trammel's child. That night, after Wolfe had tried to kill me, failed, and phoned Trammel, he'd been frantic waiting for Wolfe's next call saying Felicity's body was buried, that she was safely out of Greenhaven and there was no longer anything to fear.

But instead a frightened Dixon phoned him, told him I'd killed Wolfe, and that she didn't know if Felicity's body was still in Greenhaven. Only Trammel and Wolfe knew where the grave was. Trammel knew, because that Sunday afternoon he'd dug the grave himself, then phoned its location to Wolfe, who would bury Felicity but couldn't be gone long from Greenhaven. That explained why I'd thought there'd been too little time for Wolfe to dig a grave and then fill it again; he'd merely lowered Felicity into it and covered her with earth.

Trammel's voice got fainter and there were long pauses, but he said, "I didn't know if he'd buried her. I had to know if he'd got her out, if it was all right, no worry. Dixon . . . was worried too, and she couldn't go back to Greenhaven. We both had to know. I took her with me to the grave and the girl was there."

He began speaking more rapidly, in a garbled rush, as if he wanted to spit it all out of his bloody mouth. "Everything was all right then . . . except that Dixon knew all . . . about me. She was the only one. I . . . killed her, put her in the grave."

I could barely understand him as he told me of his long-planned resurrection, feeling the time had come to go through with it. It would tie his followers tighter when he most needed them, stop me from looking for him during at least three or four days, during which I might even have been killed—and I was the only worry left for him. A bonus was the fact that the Guardians could pin his "murder" on me, and then there were all the original reasons: money, power, the love of his followers.

His voice was a whisper when he finished. "That's all. Help me. Help me. For God's sake, don't let me die. . . ."

His eyes rolled in his head and he stared at me. I didn't say anything. His last words spilled from him in an unintelligible mumble. I stared at him unmoving, until his voice faltered and ended in a strangled cough. His head turned slightly and his eyes left mine, a clenched fist relaxed, and he was dead.

He hadn't spoken very long, but I thought he'd said enough. Enough to clear me, maybe, though I wouldn't ever be cleared in the eyes of many men. I couldn't be sure that even this would be enough.

But I looked at the still, thin body crumpled near me and I knew one thing for sure: Arthur Trammel would not rise again.

Chapter Twenty-Seven

I WAS STILL STARING at Trammel's dead body when I heard them. They walked across the floor and stopped near me as I raised my head.

There were four of them, policemen, two in uniform and two in plain clothes. Each held a gun, and one of them finally spoke. "Don't try anything, Scott. Don't move."

Another man in uniform said coldly, "Let's go, Scott."

"O. K. Will you give me a minute?"

"I'll give you a—"

"Wait a shake. Give me two minutes and I'll stand you on your heads. Trammel told me before he died of how he lied about me—about everything. Even how he worked his resurrection. It's on tape here."

I think the resurrection bit was what they were most curious about. They hesitated, and I kept it going. "Hell, he planned it years ago, when he first hit the revival trail, figured out how it could be worked, how he could swing it. When he came to L.A. he picked his Guardians and selected a doctor and a lawyer, to make sure there'd be no snags—even a mortician to 'embalm' his body, keep it under cover. Greased a few palms, everything figured out years ago."

One guy smacked a fist into his hand, staring at me, but they gave me my two minutes. I told them, fast, about Felicity and Trammel's other conquests, some of whom he'd sent to Greenhaven, to Wolfe and Dixon. "They did the jobs for him—and others," I said. "But he was the star customer. A year and a half ago he paid Wolfe five thousand dollars for an abortion, only that one was for a little Trammelite girl who was going to spill the beans about the All-High, so the operation had to go wrong. It did; she died. Wolfe and Dixon split the five thousand, which was expensive for an abortion but cheap to keep Trammel's name clean. Besides, the Trammelites' offerings paid for it.

"After that, Trammel had the kill—not manslaughter, but murder, cold-blooded, for money—to hold over their heads. In a way, Wolfe and Dixon had that on Trammel, too, but nobody would have taken their word against his. Anyway, they were all in on the kill together, so when Trammel ordered Wolfe to kill again, fast, he murdered Felicity."

They were listening, and my two minutes stretched into twenty, the twenty into an hour. Shortly after the police had come in they'd switched off the recorder and put handcuffs on my wrists. Now they rewound the tape and switched the recorder on again.

With Trammel lying dead at our feet, the four officers and I listened to his whispering voice, my questions and his answers, and heard his voice get weaker. In Trammel's words, with details that only he could have known, the story unfolded again. He told again of crushing Dixon's

156

skull with the shovel, and he told where she and Felicity were buried now. He told of others he'd caressed and kissed and named names—including Betha Green's. His voice faded and faltered, then he coughed and there was silence. After a minute or two the words an officer had spoken came from the speaker: "Let's go, Scott." It was quiet. Then the still unrolling tape reached the point where an officer had turned off the machine.

And suddenly, shockingly, Trammel's voice, recorded long before, burst with startling violence from the speaker, more obscene now than it had been in his life. The volume was still high and his words were shouted in the room. They came from the middle of the tape, words twisted by Trammel's then living lips, lascivious, suggestive, ugly: ". . . lusting for the flesh of the young, the innocent; for the evil sweetness of their breasts and thighs that inflame men's minds and make beasts of men—"

I shut it off.

There was shocked silence for a while. I'd told the police of these tapes, and looking at their faces now I knew that this, more than any words of mine, had convinced them of what Trammel had been.

Finally one of the officers spoke. "Let's go, Scott." The same words, but more friendly now.

It hadn't really been so long, but it seemed as if a year had passed since Arthur Trammel had died.

A lot had happened. I'd had trouble with the police, but all was finally explained. There'd been a flurry and a holler and I'd had to do a bit in the clink, but I'd done it standing on my head, since only a few of the charges, like fomenting a riot and disturbing the peace and puncturing seventeen sets of automobile tires, had stuck. And I'd had to pay for the tetrahedron-punctured tires.

But the clink bit was mainly for clobbering Sergeant Meadows and Al, who were still on the Raleigh force. I'd probably sue the Ledger eventually, and enjoy it. They had printed a front-page retraction, which appeared, ironically enough, in the same issue that carried some editorial condemnation of "character assassination." It was not written by Ira Borch, however. He had been in a hospital at the time, wondering what had hit him.

It was all over for me. I was pleasantly relaxed, reading the newspaper and drinking a bourbon-and-water highball. This is Lyn's apartment, naturally.

Lyn came tripping out of the shower, wrapped in a towel and a smile. "Hi."

"Hi."

"Ready for dinner?"

"Ready for anything."

"Ho, ho. You're a crazy man."

"That's what people keep telling me."

She winked at me and padded barefoot into the kitchen. While she clattered and hummed in there I thought of the case again. It had finally died out of the papers; it was stale now. But a lot of people hated me, including, of course, the Trammelites—who now called themselves the True Thinkers, having got rid of their old name but none of their old ideas. The Guardians were in jail but, unfortunately, still living. They were still living, but Felicity was dead.

Felicity, Trammel, Wofe, Dixon, all of them dead and buried, but when I thought of any of them now it was usually the one I'd never met. I had met some people I liked and enjoyed, though. Randy and Olive and Jo—I'd seen them all several times. And of course Lyn. Definitely Lyn.

I tried to finish the paper while Lyn finished fixing dinner, but maybe because of my thoughts about the case I couldn't get many kicks from all the good news: Critics Laud Show of Modern Art; Pope Denounces Birth Control as Sin; Teen-Age Gang Slays Businessman; Eight Take Refuge in Fifth Amendment.

I thought I heard a bell ringing, but it stopped. I listened a minute, then read on. The rest of the news was better, really exciting. There was to be a one-and-one-half-inch difference in skirt lengths this year. One of Emily Post's prototypes solemnly declared that one must remember to tilt one's soup bowl with one's left hand or something like that; mustn't drink from the bowl, I gathered. All good stuff.

I heard that bell ringing again. A little tinkling bell. I looked over my shoulder.

Lyn stood in the doorway. Her towel had slipped, and I thus knew immediately what had set off bells in my head. Then I noticed she had a small bell, a real one, in her hand, and was tinkling it.

"What the hell is that?" I asked.

"Dinner is ready."

"Served."

"Served, baloney. You can help yourself. To food, Shell, to *food*."

"Stingy!"

She smiled and shrugged—a dangerous thing to do in that towel. "The bell always means 'Come and get it.' Remember that at your peril. Now come on," she said. "Steaks'll get cold."

They didn't. They were thick rare sirloins and they were delicious. We had coffee and lazed around for an hour chatting pleasantly and happily. Finally we sat quietly until Lyn said, "Shell, what are you thinking?"

"Oh, about today's newspapers. And still thinking back, about the Trammel mess, instead of ahead."

She frowned and bit her lip. "Think ahead, then, darling, now that it's all over, what are you going to do?"

"It isn't all over, that's the hell—"

"Don't make a speech. What are you going to do?"

"I dunno. People really honest at Greenhaven?"

"Pretty honest."

"Maybe I'll go back there."

She didn't laugh. She didn't say anything. In a little while she got up and went out. A few minutes later I heard her in the bedroom. And I grinned, then I laughed and got up. I walked toward the bedroom, and I could still hear her bell, hear it tinkling.

THE END
of an Original Gold Medal Novel by
RICHARD S. PRATHER

Exciting Original Suspense Novels!

We'll be glad to send any of these never-before-published Gold Medal Books to you direct by mail.